In Total Darkness

A Murder Mystery By

Gloria Dial Hightower

Copyright © 2015 by Gloria Hightower
Third Edition
Published by Gloria Hightower

ISBN:13: 978- 1514791004
ISBN 10: 1514791005

All rights reserved. This book may not be reproduced in any form except for the inclusion of brief quotations in a review, without permission in writing from the author.

Printed in the USA

Additional copies may be obtained by writing to the following address:

9208 Pebble Beach Dr., NE
Albuquerque, NM 87111

This book is strictly a work of fiction, and to interpret it as anything else would be a mistake. It is not based on any true story. Although I have based the characters on real people that I know, the characteristics, personalities, and actions attributed to that character in this book are strictly figments of my imagination, and may not be construed to be real characteristics of any real person.

Gloria Hightower

DEDICATION

Nothing is so dear to me as my family of loved ones, Tom, Lisa, Ken, Judy, Beau and Ryan. You keep me conscious of the things in life that really matter. This book is for you.

ACKNOWLEDGMENTS

My sincere thanks for the following persons for their guidance, help, and inspiration for this book.

My husband, Tommy, for his unbiased opinion of the manuscript.

Dr. Wes Wilkening, O.D., PA for the information regarding ophthalmology.

Vicki Palmer, for her tireless editing.

Jean Chapman, for additional suggestions for improvement.

Bryce Dial, for his talent and expertise in graphic art and design of the cover and most of all his patience.

In Total Darkness

CAST OF CHARACTERS

Apodaca-Ramos, Senator Manuel Maria – NM State Senator
Benedetti, Alfred – Ava's bodyguard
Bertha – Nicolette's Nanny
Cadrigan III, Michael Thomas "Trey" – Nicolette's son
Cadrigan, Michael – Nicolette's third husband
Carmen – Pete Lucero's ex-wife
Cherry – Head bookkeeper at Howell Carpets
Chuck – Waiter at Rio Grande Country Club
Ciccone, Dr. Antonio – Local gynecologist
Diane – Ginger's golfing buddy
Dotti - Ginger's golfing buddy
Du Pree, Nicolette - Drop-dead gorgeous waitress RGCC
Grissom, Ava – Saudi Arabian Bank of Belgium Rep.
Harrigan, Richard – Nicolette's rich second husband
Harris – Computer technician hired by Howell Carpets
Howell, Brandon – Tom's grandson, Jon's son
Howell, Sydney – Tom's granddaughter, Jon's daughter
Howell, Jonathan "J" – Tom's youngest grandson
Howell, Ginger – Tom's wife
Howell, Jon – Tom & Ginger's son
Howell, Judith – Jon's wife
Howell, Tom – Owner of Howell Carpets, President RGCC
Janette – Tom's personal assistant
Jean – Ginger's golfing buddy
Johnson, Pamela – Alcoholic widow of local veterinarian
Katy – Ladies Locker Room Attendant RGCC
Lucero, Pete – Homicide Detective APD
Lucero, Pete Jr. and Rosie – Detective Lucero's children
Mahoney, Patrick – Homicide Detective, Pete's partner
McGuire, Grant – Tom's old college roommate
O'Grady, Robert – Nicolette's first husband
Paula – Waitress at RGCC
Ricky the Rat—Local police informant
Rosalie – Ginger's golfing buddy
Simpson, Bud – Lobbyist & Member RGCC
Simpson, Claire – Bud's unsuspecting wife
Stephens, Mike – Asst. Manager at RGCC

Prologue

I can't open my eyes or else I have gone blind!

She was lying down on a hard surface and was stiff from being cold. She rubbed her arms briskly to get some feeling back into them.

It was totally dark. There was not even a pinpoint of light in the small room in which she lay. She raised her fingers toward her face, but could not make out the shape of her hand. Gradually coming out of the drug stupor, she began to panic.

Where am I? What has happened to me?

She cautiously turned on one elbow and raised her head slightly. With the other hand she reached out slowly, groping for anything that might be in front of her. She knew that she had her eyes open, but there was only total darkness.

Panic rose in her mind and she tried her voice. "HELP!" she croaked. "Somebody please help me!" She listened for a response, but the silence was as thick as the darkness. Not a sound. Total blackness.

Where am I? Could I be dead? Is this what death is like?

In Total Darkness

Chapter One

Tom was standing at the window with his hands jammed into his pockets, not moving a muscle, staring into space. He had no clue that his comfortable life was about to be turned topsy-turvy.

Ginger Howell needed her husband's signature on the legal form she had just completed. She walked across the hall to Tom's office and through the open door.

"Something interesting out there?" she asked.

Startled, Tom replied, "Oh! No, I was just rehearsing the speech that I have to give at Rio Grande Country Club tonight."

"Sorry to bother you, my love, but I need your John Henry on these papers."

Tom Howell moved with the grace of a natural athlete as he walked over to his desk and sat down. He reached for the pipe that was in the ashtray—then thought about it and reached for a pen instead. He wasn't extremely tall, just about six feet, and still wore his dark blond hair in the "flat-top" style. Even though he and Ginger had been married for over forty years he had maintained the physical attributes of a much younger man. Tom was a competent administrator and kept the Howell Carpet store running smoothly. His keen blue eyes never missed whatever was going on around him and he had the natural tact to keep all of the many employees happy and productive. "Now what are these papers all about?"

"Nothing to worry about, just sign them!" replied Ginger. She sat down in the tall burgundy guest chair in front of his executive desk. Ginger had worked alongside her husband for all the years of their marriage and they were still the best of friends. She had glossy brown hair streaked nicely with strands of silver, complementing her dark brown eyes. She had maintained her figure by diet and exercise over the years. Long dark lashes surrounded her eyes that sparkled with interest in almost everything around her. "How about you run through your speech and let me hear it," she continued.

"I am not really excited about doing this, you know. Why don't they do something else for their entertainment," he complained.

"You know as well as I do that the President is expected to give this speech at the annual meeting. The *President's Overlook* is a tradition."

Tom groaned. "I just don't like public speaking. I'm always afraid of making a fool of myself."

"That's not going to happen," she smiled. "You will be just fine. Your tuxedo and formal wear is all laid out at home, so all you need to do is shower and change."

"That's another thing. That monkey-suit! This is one tradition I could live without."

"It doesn't last that long, and you'll do just fine with the speech. Want to let me hear it?"

"Well, okay. I guess I do need to do it aloud," he grumbled and began to rehearse it aloud.

***

Chapter Two

Grant McGuire groaned as he struggled to sit up. He ran his hand over his face, as if to check and make sure it was still connected to his head. Horrible pounding. His head throbbed with the worst headache he could remember.

"I've got to quit taking those pills," he mumbled aloud. The yo-yo of uppers to waken and downers to go to sleep, along with recreational drugs and alcohol, was taking its toll. He frowned with the effort of willing his aching body to rise from the bed and reach for the crumpled pack of cigarettes on his nightstand. His hands shook as he flipped the lighter and finally touched it to the end of the tobacco. He savored the first drag of smoke as he drew it deeply into his lungs, then almost collapsed into a fit of coughing.

"Ooohh, Mercy that hurts!" he mumbled and glanced over at the empty beer cans that littered the top of the dresser. "You'd think that I would have learned by now when to stop."

He groaned as he stumbled into the bathroom for his daily constitution: brush his teeth, shave, and take a steaming hot shower.

As the hot water beat a staccato on his dark salt and pepper hair, he thought about all the things that were wrong with his life. "There's just been too much. Too much of everything...except money!" Excesses of drugs, alcohol, gambling, and women only accentuated the financial mess he had made of his life. He had turned to drug dealing to solve a severe cash flow problem, and now he was in so deep there didn't seem to be a way to climb out. It just wasn't fair. "If I had the money that Tom Howell has stacked up, then maybe I could straighten out my life, quit drinking and doing drugs…even make an impression on that beautiful girl I met." He squinted and frowned as he thought about Tom.

A pattern of always being in second place had started when his father always bragged on his older brother, while pointing out his failures. His brother was taller, more handsome, more athletic, kinder, smarter, and more talented. His brother could do no wrong, while he couldn't walk and chew gum at the same time to hear his father tell it. Not only that, but every time he found a girl he really liked, she invariably fell for his brother.

Now, years later, his best friend, Tom Howell, had taken the place of his brother by beating him at everything he tried. He had met Tom during his first semester in college when they were assigned to be roommates. They shared a lot more than just a room. They studied for the same tests together, took turns doing the laundry and cleaning the room, double-dated on occasion, and played on the same football team. After college, the friendship had remained, but their lives took divergent paths. Tom had been married to the same beautiful woman for over forty years, while he had been divorced four times. Tom's children were good-looking, intelligent, and successful, while his four children had three different mothers, struggled in school, and one of them bordered on mental retardation. Tom Howell had been elected president of Rio Grande Country Club, an office that he wanted so badly he could taste it. When Tom Howell opened his carpet store it had immediately become a financial blockbuster, while he had filed for reorganization in bankruptcy court for the second time in his life. To top all of this off, he played golf every Wednesday afternoon with Tom Howell and not once had he ever beaten Tom's score. Tom Howell was his best friend—and he despised him. It just wasn't fair. Some way, somehow, he would make Tom Howell pay—suffer the way he suffered.

Stepping out of the shower, a thought began to germinate deep within his devious mind. He *could* make Tom Howell suffer! The blackness that consumed his mind settled into place as he figured how he could make a simple start and gradually drive Tom Howell into frustration and then perhaps a nervous breakdown—a state of mind with which he had become increasingly familiar.

He dressed quickly and picked up the stack of mail that was on the hall table. He hadn't looked at it in a week or more, electing not to be reminded of all the unpaid bills. Surely there would be an envelope there from Publisher's Clearing House and a few solicitations for credit cards from various sources. It wasn't much of a nuisance for Tom Howell, but it was a start. He quickly filled out the application and added about forty of the magazine stickers. He realized that he would need to find some credit card solicitations with Tom's name already on them—maybe from the trash can at Tom's office, or at his home, if they hadn't gotten into the habit of shredding everything yet. He laughed as he visualized the mailbox at the Howell estate!

***

In Total Darkness

Chapter Three

Nicolette du Pree was drop-dead gorgeous. Her heritage was Irish, and she had flaming red hair, creamy ivory skin, and emerald green eyes—which made her stand out in any crowd. Her grandfather on her father's side was French, giving her the name du Pree, but everyone else in her family was full-fledged Irish. She was a little over five-foot eight; tall enough that she could have become a model if she had not been so curvaceous. The long red curls that framed her heart-shaped face and the perfect bow of her lips gave her an angelic appearance. Appearances however, can be deceiving.
Nicolette was far from angelic.

She had been called Nicki from the cradle, and her fiery spirit had kept her in trouble most of her twenty-seven years. She had been known to swear like a backwoodsman on occasion, smoked thin little brown cigarillos, and could hold more liquor than most men…and she had drunk a lot of liquor with a lot of different men recently.

"Ay, lassie, the gent at the end o' the bar does remind me a bit o' my first husband, Robert O'Grady." said Nicki in her exaggerated Irish brogue. She only used it when she was teasing or trying to be humorous.

"Oh really?" replied Paula, the other waitress. "And just how is that?"

"He's thinkin' that he's God's gift to all women, but ye

don't think God would play a trick like that on us, now do ye?" The girls both laughed, and Nicki dropped the brogue. "Robert O'Grady was my high school sweetheart, the first man in my life, and I was in love with love. But to be honest with you, I married him primarily to get out from under my father's strict thumb."

"Your father was that strict?" asked Paula.

"Oh, yes. And he was a lot smarter than I gave him credit for at the time, too. Robert and I were so poor the church mice had to give hand-outs to us." The girls laughed again. "That was probably why I was so ready for a change when I met this rich widower. Robbie and I had been married about two years, and along came this older man. He was rich, poised, and wise to the world, but most important — lonely. His wife had died a couple of years before. It was easy for me to become friends with him, and he treated me like a real lady."

"What was his name?"

"Richard Harrigan, but I probably should have called him King Midas—he was that rich—and he really wanted me. Poor Robert didn't understand, but agreed to the divorce. I think he was pretty broken up about it, at least for a while."

"How did Mr. Harrigan get so rich? Did he inherit the money from his Pa?"

"No, he made his fortune by buying and selling real estate." Nicki looked down at the end of the bar and said in full "brogue mode", "I think I need to refill the wee laddie's cup agin'."

When she returned, Paula asked her, "Well, what happened then? Did he ask you to marry him, or just move in with him?"

"Richard Harrigan was not the "moving-in-with" type. We were married in Paris about six months after we met, and you wouldn't believe our honeymoon!" She paused, and then said, "Richard bought me designer clothes, an expensive car, incredible jewelry, and took me on vacations to the best resorts in the world. He was a wee bit older than my father, and I think he felt the gifts would make up for the difference in our ages."

"So you married this rich old man, and here you are waiting tables in a country club lounge? What happened? Did you have to sign a prenuptial agreement, or did you just get tired of the old fellow?"

Nicki frowned. "I would never have gotten tired of that goose. Too many golden eggs. I guess I got a little too rambunctious for him one night. He had a massive heart attack and died."

"And you lost everything?"

"Well, much to the chagrin of his extended family, Richard had changed his will and left his entire estate to me, except for most of his first wife's personal things and some token bequests to his children. They weren't too happy about it at all. Called me a few unkind names, to say the least."

"Wow, your story is better than watching soap operas. You inherited all that money, but how did you lose it?"

Nicki suddenly became very agitated, frowned, and shook her head. "I think we'd better start getting these tables set up for the meeting and dinner-dance tonight, don't you."

Every time Nicki started thinking about Michael it felt as if she had been kicked in the stomach. To even think about his infidelity made her physically sick to her stomach, and the loss of the money she had inherited just added insult to injury. She brooded about it as she began setting up the tables for dinner.

The period of mourning following Richard's death didn't last long. Once she met Michael, she lost her heart. Suddenly the sun rose and the sun set with Michael Cadrigan. She began to think of vine-covered white cottages, two or three children, and roses in the front yard. By this time Nicki was twenty-two and if anything, had only grown more beautiful with each passing year. Having Richard's money gave her the freedom to choose expensive clothes, go to the most exclusive hairdressers, and employ housekeepers and a personal assistant. Michael Cadrigan was everything that Nicki had ever imagined that she would want in a man. A little over six feet, his healthy tan set off the sun-streaked blonde hair, the dark blue eyes, and the very white teeth that showed when he flashed the smile that would melt any girl's heart. He had been a professional tennis player in his younger days, and after retiring from competition had become a top rated tennis instructor.

Nicki fell head over heels in love with Michael and he seemed to be very much in love with her. They honeymooned on the French Riviera and decided to make their home in Miami. Michael felt that he had to continue working, even though it wasn't a financial necessity with the millions that Nicki had inherited from Richard's estate.

Within a year, they were blessed with a beautiful baby boy and decided to name him after his father and grandfather, making his name Michael Thomas Cadrigan, III. They nicknamed him "Trey". Nicki had never been happier in her life. When Trey was two years old Nicki became pregnant again, and this was about the time her life started to unravel.

Michael developed a real love of the soft life that Nicki's money afforded him. He also developed a love of gambling. He became addicted, and lost huge amounts of money on flying trips to Atlanta and Las Vegas. He continued to give tennis lessons, but only as an excuse to get out of the house. Michael met lots of conniving people at the gambling tables, and easily became a victim of scurrilous real estate developers. Before they were through with him, Michael had lost all of the millions that Nicki had inherited. She had given him full control of her finances, trusting him completely. By the time the money was gone, Michael had undergone a complete personality change. He was moody, with bouts of deep depression and irritability, and was drinking heavily. He stopped coming home after his tennis lessons, and instead began to hang out in the lounge at the resort complex where he worked. To make matters worse, Nicki's pregnancy had become difficult. With three months to go before the baby was due, her doctor prescribed complete bed rest to keep her from a miscarriage.

She tried everything that she could think of to pacify the husband that she adored so much, but it was really distressing under the circumstances. If Nicki said anything at all to Michael about his drinking or not coming home, he would fly into a rage and scream at her until she dissolved into tears. Michael's drinking friends soon introduced him to the world of forgetfulness, all wrapped up in a little package of white powder. Cocaine.

All of these memories flooded Nicki's mind as she went about the business of placing the napkins and silverware around the tables. As if in a dream, she relived that horrible scene the night that Michael came home with another woman....

Nicki pushed the buzzer by her bed that would summon her housekeeper, Bertha. It was only a moment before Bertha hurried into the bedroom.

"Yes, Mrs. Cadrigan, how may I be of help?" asked Bertha.

"Oh, Bertie, I was just wondering if Michael had returned home?" asked Nicki.

"I think so. I was in the other part of the house with Trey, but I thought I heard voices in the entry. Would you like me to check for you?"

"No. That's all right. You shouldn't be away from Trey for very long. I haven't been out of bed all day, and I really think that I need to walk a little bit. Would you please bring my dressing tray over to the bed? I would like to freshen up a wee mite."

Bertha rolled the little table closer to the bed. It had a washbasin, cloth, mirror, hairbrush, and all of Nicki's make-up.

"Thanks, Bertie, I can handle it from here. You go ahead and get back to the nursery. Trey may need you."

Nicki pulled the brush through her long red hair. She then

applied make-up to cover the dark circles that were under the emerald green eyes. She added mascara to her long, thick eyelashes and a touch of blush to her cheeks. Surveying her work in the mirror, she decided that she was ready to see her husband. Swinging her legs over the edge of the bed, she held onto the bedpost, and pulled herself to her feet. She had not gained much weight with this pregnancy, even at six months, but the threat of a miscarriage was very real.

Michael had entered the house with a lady friend, both of them under the influence of alcohol and cocaine.

"Shhh. Don't wanna wake the ol' lady," Michael slurred. The girl giggled, but didn't reply.

"We'll use the guest bedroom. That way Nicki won't hear us coming up the stairs."

"Sounds okay to me," she replied. "I'm not sure I could make it up the stairs, anyway." She giggled again, and then said, "Ooh, what a pretty place ya got here, Mikey."

They stumbled their way into the guest bedroom and clumsily began stripping off each other's clothes.

Nicki slowly walked to the top of the stairs, not sure at all if she could make it all the way to the bottom. Carefully holding onto the railing, she negotiated the stairs one little step at a time. She wanted Michael to be surprised at how well she looked. When she reached the bottom she held onto the wall for support and followed the boisterous sounds coming from the guest suite. She wasn't prepared for what she saw when she opened the door. The shock of seeing her beloved husband having sex with another woman was like being hit by a locomotive. Wordlessly, she turned and tried to run back up the stairs. About halfway up the stairs she felt a sharp pain and the flow of blood and amniotic fluid before she passed out.

Three weeks after Nicki lost the baby, she had sold the house, filed for divorce, packed up Trey and Bertha and what few belongings they would need and moved to Albuquerque,

New Mexico. It had taken most of the proceeds from the sale of the house to clear up the debts Michael had incurred. She didn't see him again after that horrible night, and never wanted to lay eyes on him again. She would start over, and this time, *she* would be the one breaking the hearts. No one would ever get close enough to hurt her like this again.

She introduced herself in Albuquerque as Nicolette du Pree, going back to her maiden name. Trey was young enough that he would never remember that his last name had been Cadrigan.
 Finding a job as a waitress had been easy. The Rio Grande Country Club jumped at the chance to hire her when she applied. It was a way for her to meet wealthy men and earn enough to make a living for herself and Trey.

Nicki rubbed her forehead as if to wipe away all the memories of her life with Michael Cadrigan. She had loved him so deeply and had been hurt so badly! Trying to forget, it had been easy for her to slip into the abuse of alcohol, and when that had not been enough, she too had turned to drugs. Right now, she really needed to be able to forget. She would have to wait until after the dinner, until she had her break. She would call her source to meet her in the ladies' locker room while she was on break. The other thing that was bothering her, and had her scared for her life, didn't have anything to do with her past.
 Nicki had overheard a conversation that could ruin a lot of people. She wasn't sure they knew she had overheard them, and it was scary to think what they might do to keep her from passing on that conversation to the right people.

Damn! I need a smoke, and I need that fix! But I've made up my mind. I'm going to kick this nasty habit. Tonight will be the last hit."

***

In Total Darkness

Chapter Four

Tom Howell frowned as he tried to manipulate the bow tie into place. He clenched his teeth, unaware that his displeasure was so apparent.

"You *really* aren't looking forward to tonight, are you?" asked his wife, Ginger.

"How can you tell?" asked Tom as he adjusted his tuxedo shirt and turned to look at her. "By the way, you look stunning!" he said as he checked out the dinner dress she wore. "It's too bad that *you* aren't the main speaker tonight instead of me." He ran his fingers through his dark blond hair. The streaks of gray at his temples tended to make him look more distinguished than older, and the habit of running his fingers through his hair was totally an unconscious one.

Ginger applied the last touches of her lipstick and said, "I don't think the membership at Rio Grande Country Club would accept a speech from the *wife* of the president, Sweetheart." She turned to the full-length mirror, frowned briefly at the small strands of silver in her dark brown hair, adjusted her skirt over her slender hips, and giving her hair a final pat, said, "That's it. Are you ready to go?" Before Tom could answer her, the phone rang. He shrugged and turned to answer it as Ginger reached for her evening wrap.

"Hello," said Tom, answering the phone call. Ginger watched as Tom raised his eyebrows in surprise. "Of course, Nicki, I'll be happy to meet with you. Will you be at the meeting and dinner-dance tonight? Oh! I understand. Then why don't you give me a call in the morning and we'll arrange for a time and place. I understand that it's important, and that no one else must know." He paused, "Overheard what? Okay, you can tell me all about it in the morning. Ginger won't say a word, I promise. Okay, I'll look for your call in the morning." Tom was rather puzzled as he hung up the phone.

"That was *our* Nicki? The drop-dead-gorgeous-red-headed-waitress from the club? What on earth does she want to talk to you about…. or are you her next target?" Ginger smiled as she teased her husband of more than forty years.

"Now, Ginger, cut that out." said Tom. "She seemed to be very upset, and said that it was not only important, but dangerous for her to be talking to me."

"*Dangerous?*" queried Ginger, her brown eyes sparkling with mischief. "That's strange. You don't think that her call has anything to do with all these weird things that have been happening to you the past few weeks, do you?"

"Who knows?" replied Tom. "But if ordering thirty or forty magazine subscriptions in someone else's name, and applying for in-store credit cards at locations all over town in someone else's name is dangerous, then I guess it might have something to do with it. Nancy has been working full time on the phone just to get all this stuff cancelled." said Tom, referring to the receptionist at Howell Carpets.

"I can't imagine someone with that much extra time on their hands." Ginger paused and then said, "We'd better go. It's takes twenty minutes to get to the club, and you don't want to be late."

The ride to Rio Grande Country Club was a much shorter distance than the couple used to drive when they were members at Four Hills Country Club, which was a big factor in their making the change. This particular ride was rather quiet in the Howell car, as Tom and Ginger seemed to be lost in thought. Tom was reviewing the speech he had written, and Ginger was puzzling over this telephone call from Nicolette du Pree.

Finally Ginger couldn't stand it anymore. "Okay. It's none of my business, but Nicki's reputation is one of tumbling from one relationship to the next, with little concern for the welfare of anyone who gets in her way." She stole a glance at her handsome husband who was intent upon his driving as well as the speech. "I've been trying to think about the last time anyone talked about Nicki. Rumor was that she had been married when she was younger and had a little boy, but divorced her husband when she caught him cheating on her."

"Yeah, that's about the same story I've heard in the men's locker room. But now the story is that there have been affairs with several men, including Mike Stevens, Dr. Antonio Ciccone, and Bud Simpson."

"I am surprised that it is allowed for one of the assistant managers at the club to be carrying on with another employee. I heard that Mike was married at the time, and the father of a couple of children. As far as Dr. Ciccone, well, he's a single physician with the reputation of being a notorious womanizer. And of course I know Bud Simpson. I just met his wife, Claire, at bridge the other day."

"There probably have been others. Nicki is young, probably mid to late twenties."

"Yes, and being fairly tall with a stunning figure, those dark green eyes and that thick, curly, mane of red hair, it's impossible for anyone to not notice Nicki du Pree."

"The guys say she is very athletic and plays a pretty good game of golf when the opportunity arises. Unfortunately, she is sexually promiscuous, drinks to excess, and the last rumors were that she has been experimenting with drugs."

"I've heard most of that as well. Several women at the club would gladly string her from the tallest cottonwood tree on the course, but there are more men in the club who enjoy having her around just for the eye-candy." Knowing these things about Nicki made Ginger even more curious about why she would want to set up an appointment with Tom. "Well, I guess we'll find out in the morning what she has on her mind. It's the "dangerous" word that has me curious."

They pulled into the drop off area at the front door of Rio Grande Country Club. The building was very new, and sported huge glass windows over the entire front. The canopied front door opened into a two-story atrium with an enormous crystal chandelier gracing the center of the lobby. Three connecting fountains gurgled with flowing water, which was colored to match whatever event was happening at the club. Tonight the water was in streams of red, white, and blue, to celebrate Labor Day. The balcony surrounding the lobby was covered with crystal-rope lighting that glistened like diamonds and further enhanced the luxurious decor of the lobby. A curved stairway flowed from the lobby up to the double doors of the ballroom, reminiscent of the ante-bellum mansions from *Gone with the Wind*. The elegance was almost palpable, and one could see each person entering the lobby walk a little taller and straighter.

Tom pitched the car keys to the valet when they pulled up to the canopied front door of the country club. They stopped to check Ginger's evening wrap with the coatroom attendant, then Tom took Ginger's elbow to escort her up the curved staircase to the ballroom. As they entered the ballroom they found the seats about two-thirds full for the meeting.

"I think there is still enough time to get a cup of coffee before the meeting begins," said Tom.

"Would you like a cup, or a Dr Pepper? Or a glass of wine?" he asked.

"I don't think so. You go right ahead and do your thing. I'll be just fine, besides, I'll bet our son and his family are already here." replied Ginger. Just then she glanced across the room and saw their son, Jon, and his wife, Judith coming through the ballroom door.

"Hi, kids," she said, approaching the handsome couple. Jon was tall with an athletic build, dark blond hair, and blue eyes, much like his father. He looked very professional and prosperous in his tuxedo. Judith was petite. She might reach five feet tall and weighed about a hundred pounds. Her light brown eyes were enormous, and were veiled with long, thick, dark lashes, matching her sun-streaked dark hair. They were smiling and comfortable together, holding hands. "Where's the rest of your clan?" asked Ginger.

"Hello, Mom," replied Jon. "I think that Brandon and Jonathan went to the snack bar. They are always hungry! Where did Sydney go, Judith?" he asked his wife.

"Oh, you know Sydney, she had to check out her make-up one last time," replied Judith.

Jon and Judith doted on their three teenaged children. Brandon had just turned seventeen. He was the ultimate athlete. About six feet tall, black hair, dark brown eyes, and smooth fair skin. Sydney was the second child, and a virtual copy of her mother, except for having blue eyes. She was sixteen, petite, athletic, and vivacious. Her personality made her a natural as a cheerleader, and her size made her the girl that always got thrown into the air and was the top of the pyramid. Jon was fiercely protective of his daughter, and was anticipating fighting boys off with a stick. The younger son, Jonathan, had his father's middle name, but liked the nickname of "J". His eyes were like his mother's, light brown, which exactly matched the color of his hair and his olive complexion. At fourteen, he had already distinguished himself as a champion wrestler, as well as playing both offense and defense on the freshman football team. Both Brandon and "J" spent a lot of extra time on the football field and were getting quite proficient at kicking as well as handling their other football positions. Ginger was quite sure that each of her three grandchildren could hang the moon.

"Dad went to grab a last shot of coffee. I think that he is a bit more nervous about this speech tonight than he is willing to admit," stated Ginger. "We might want to go ahead and grab a good seat. It looks like it is going be a full house tonight. We can save three extra chairs for the kids."

Ginger surveyed the room after they were seated. She saw Dr. Ciccone seated two rows in front of her, along with several of her golfing buddies and their husbands. A flash of flaming red hair caught her attention as she happened to see Nicolette du Pree carrying a tray full of drinks toward a corner of the lounge. Once again the questions bubbled up in her mind, but realizing that nothing would be said until the next day, she turned her attention to the room full of elegantly dressed people.

"Wow, who in the world is that?" whispered Judith. She had noticed a middle-aged woman enter the room, accompanied by a rough looking man. The woman was not very tall, had peroxided blonde hair, and was wearing a two-piece outfit in gold and silver silk. It was quite apparent that she was wearing false eyelashes, and the fake fingernails on her hands accentuated the fact that she was dripping with diamonds. The man with her appeared to be a bodyguard. He was about six-two, two-hundred-forty pounds, barrel-chested, black hair, mustache, dark heavy eyebrows over brown eyes, and was heavily muscled. One could tell that he spent a lot of time in a gymnasium, working out. He looked uncomfortable in the rented tuxedo he wore, and the neck of his shirt looked at least one size too small. The frown he wore affirmed that he was uncomfortable.

"I've never seen her before in my life," responded Ginger.

"Nothing to spice up the night like a mysterious stranger, is there? We'll ask Tom when he finishes his speech."

"Good evening, Mrs. Howell. You are looking particularly beautiful this evening." Ginger turned to see Mike Stevens, the assistant manager of the club. Mike was thirty-five, medium height, with just the beginning of "love handles" appearing around his waist. A hint of a double chin was hidden by a neatly trimmed beard. He took Ginger's hand and patted it briefly.

"Mike. Good evening. I'm looking forward to the dinner-dance more than the meeting. I've already heard Tom's speech. Have you met my son and his wife? This is Jon Howell and his wife Judith. My three grandchildren will be joining us shortly. Kids, this is Mike Stevens, one of our club managers."

"I'm sure that I've seen Jon on the tee box, haven't I?" asked Mike.

"You might say that I'm a wannabee." quipped Jon. "I want-to-be out on the course more often than my business allows me to be."

"What is your business, Mr. Howell?" asked Mike.

"Please call me Jon. Mr. Howell is my father," he requested. "I'm a custom home builder. I've been in the construction business for over twenty years."

"My word! You must have started in the business when you were in elementary school."

"Not quite. But I have a quite a few projects under my belt. If you are in the market for a new home, give me a call."

"Do you also work in commercial construction? We have a couple of projects in the works for the club. Would you be interested in bidding on them?" asked Mike.

"Of course. I have completed several commercial jobs, and would be glad to take a look at what you are planning. Here's my business card. Give me a call when you'd like to talk about it," said Jon, handing him the card.

"I will surely do that. Now I've got to get up to the stage to make some introductions. Nice meeting you and your wife, Jon." Before Mike could head for the stage, Ginger pulled him aside.

"Mike, who is the lady in the third row up in front of us? You see the one I'm talking about? The blond lady with the rough looking man seated beside her? I don't think that I've ever seen her before," she asked quietly. Mike looked up front.

"Oh, yes," he replied, keeping his voice low. "That's Ava Grissom, and her companion, Alfred Benedetti. She joined our club about a week ago. And now I really must go."

"Of course, Mike, and thanks."

"He seemed very nice, Ginger," said Judith.

"Well, he puts up a good front for someone with a broken heart," replied Ginger.

"That sounds intriguing. Who broke his heart?" Judith asked.

"All the talk was that he was head over heels in love with Nicolette du Pree. He left his wife and family, moved in with her and was ready to adopt her little boy, from the talk in the clubhouse. The next thing we heard was that she had kicked him out and that Dr. Ciccone had moved in with her," stated Ginger.

"Mom, that sounds like a lot of rumors. Are you sure of your facts?" asked Jon.

"You are right, of course, Jon. I shouldn't be spreading tales," replied his mother. "By the way, Judith, that's Dr. Ciccone just returning to his seat in front of us. He is the older gentleman with the silver gray hair, wearing the powder blue tuxedo."

Antonio Ciccone mesmerized any woman within speaking distance. He was just under six feet tall and had piercing gray-blue eyes. His full head of prematurely gray hair was complimented by a fastidiously groomed short beard and mustache. When he spoke, people were surprised at the deep bass tones of his voice. His hands were definitely the hands of a physician, with well-trimmed nails shiny with clear nail polish. Women threw themselves at him at any opportunity, giving him a well-earned reputation as a womanizer.

"Oh. Of course. Now I recognize him. He is one of the doctors at the clinic where I go," said Judith. "Doesn't he specialize in gynecology and obstetrics?"

"I think so." Ginger stopped. "Well, look who just blew in

and sat down beside him. It's our very own Grant McGuire and his "girl du jour". I wonder where Grant found this one? She looks young enough to be his daughter. Very pretty, though, isn't she?" said Ginger. Grant always walked as if he were dancing, although his drug and alcohol habits made him a bit shaky tonight. He was not particularly good looking, but took infinite pains with grooming, and always wore well-tailored fashionable clothes. His formal wear tonight was selected to enhance the color of his salt and pepper hair. Bushy eyebrows topped his eyes, which always seemed to carry a mischievous secret. His mustache was also bushy, and probably was grown to cover a rather straight, weak mouth. The word to describe his date was most likely to be "bimbo". She was very beautiful, with soft creamy skin, long honey-blonde hair, and very blue eyes. Unfortunately, a conversation with her would probably reveal that there was a minimum of gray matter between her nicely shaped ears.

"Hmmm. I think that I've seen this girl before. Honey, do you recognize her?" Jon asked his wife.

"She really does look familiar, but I can't remember just now where we might have seen her. Oh, isn't she the hostess at the Chili Bean Café?" replied Judith.

"Well, good evening, Ginger." Ginger turned toward the voice. It was Pamela Johnson. Pamela had been widowed for about a year, and seemed to fill most of her time since then becoming very well-acquainted with bottles of Scotch. Her words were slightly slurred now. Weaving slightly, she braced herself by holding onto the back of Ginger's chair. The more she drank, the more inclined she was to talk, and the more she talked, the louder her voice. Realizing that Pamela was well on her way, Ginger gracefully stood up, grasped Pamela by the elbow, and started walking with her to an empty seat.

"Pamela, dear. How good of you to stop by and say hello. You know that Tom is giving the *President's Outlook* tonight, don't you? I think that he's about ready to begin. Will this seat be comfortable for you?" Ginger maneuvered Pamela into an empty chair, right beside Bud Simpson and his wife Claire. She bent over and whispered into Bud's ear, "Take care of Pamela for us, at least until after Tom's speech, all right, Bud?" Bud nodded and Ginger slipped back to her seat.

Tom Howell had unconsciously sipped from his coffee cup as he concentrated on his notes. He looked at his watch and decided to make one last "pit stop". When he returned from the men's room, he took one last big swig of coffee, and frowned bitterly. "Chuck, that's the nastiest tasting coffee that I've ever had! You might want to pour it out and brew a fresh pot. Phew!" He checked his watch again, then picked up his notes and walked toward the stage in the front of the ballroom. His stomach had begun to roll, which surprised him. He didn't think he was that nervous, and subconsciously tried to remember what he had eaten for lunch.

Rio Grande Country Club was nestled along the river in the North Valley, closer to Corrales than to downtown and was relatively new to the Albuquerque scene. Many of the members of the historic Albuquerque Country Club had moved their membership after this club opened, as they wanted to enjoy the elegance of the new buildings and escape the huge assessment that was to be levied at ACC. Tom Howell made his way through the ballroom toward the short flight of stairs that led to an elevated stage area where the podium awaited him. He realized that the rolling of his stomach was increasing. Just as he reached the top of the stairs, the impulse to throw up hit him full force. He turned and ran to the men's room before vomiting violently into the toilet. Chuck, the waiter in the lounge, followed him offering help.

There was a stir in the ballroom as the assembled guests began buzzing about Tom's flight. Ginger and Jon quickly retreated to the back of the ballroom, with Jon going into the men's room to check on his Dad. Dr. Ciccone followed Jon, offering his services as a medical doctor.

Five minutes passed before Dr. Ciccone appeared.

"Ginger, I would bet my bottom dollar that Tom has been given an emetic medicine," he said.

"Come on, Tony, English, please!" cried Ginger.

"Symptoms show signs that Tom ingested ipecac, which is …"

"I know what ipecac is!" interrupted Ginger. "My question is, what do we do about it now, and how serious is it?"

"It is not serious at all, except that Tom will be throwing up for the next half hour or so. He may feel rotten, maybe some mild diarrhea, drowsiness, but it is not life threatening. We *prescribe* ipecac when patients ingest something toxic, to quickly get it out of their systems. Of course I'd have to know that the substance did not contain something like drain cleaner, which can do as much damage coming up as going down, and…"

"Tony!" cried Ginger. "I don't need a lecture, just tell me what to do with Tom right now."

"Oh, well, he would probably be just fine lying down in the men's locker room, close to the johns for about half an hour, then he should be well enough to make the trip home," intoned Dr. Anthony Ciccone, in his most professional deep bass tone of voice.

Just then, Jon came out of the restroom.

"Mom, Dad said to give you his notes, that you had heard him rehearse his speech several times, and could probably go ahead and give the speech for him. Chuck and I are taking him down to the men's locker room to lie down," instructed Jon.

"But…" Ginger began.

"Now don't argue, Mom! Dad said that you would argue, and to insist that you don't let the team down. Go give Dad's speech." Jon put the notes in his mother's hand and returned to the restroom. With no one left to whom she could protest, Ginger took a deep breath and walked back into the ballroom, up the stairs, and to the podium.

She took deep breath, "Well, as you saw, there's many a slip twixt the cup and the lip." She waited for the chuckling to stop, and then said, "I knew that Tom really was reluctant to give this speech tonight, but I had no idea that he would "invent" a virulent stomach virus in order to avoid it. Actually, I have read Tom's speech and have heard him rehearse it, so if you will bear with me, I hope I can at least make a stab at relaying the information Tom wanted to pass on to you folks tonight." Ginger spent the next half-hour giving the members as much of Tom's speech as she could remember.

The ballroom at Rio Grande Country Club was on the second floor of the building. Nicki du Pree took her fifteen-minute break and headed down the back stairs to the ladies' locker room. Her hands had begun to shake as the drug she had taken before work was wearing off.

"Damn! My source had just better show up," she thought as she flipped on the locker room light. Then she flipped it off again, thinking that a drug source just might prefer the dark. "Hello? Anybody here?" she called.

Silence. She could hear the ticking of the old clock in the adjacent card room.

"Damn!" She flopped down in one of the upholstered easy chairs in the lounge area, propped her feet up on the coffee table, and said to the empty room, "I only have fifteen minutes; you damned well better hurry it up." Nicki patted her foot, and then drummed her long bright red fingernails on the arm of the chair as the need for the drug crawled up her spine and made her hands begin to tremble. She lit a cigarillo, took a deep drag, then slowly blew out the smoke. Little drops of perspiration were forming on her forehead. Five more minutes passed before she heard footsteps entering the darkened room.

"Nicki?" softly said a deep voice.

"Yeah. In here. I thought you'd never come, or had forgotten."

In Total Darkness

"I have a special surprise for you tonight. It works a lot quicker than coke does. Shoot it directly into the vein. Instant high. What about it?"

Nicki could barely make out the shape of her source in the dark. She didn't much like the idea of needles, but she needed the fix badly. Her distaste for the entire situation rose in her mouth. She hated needing drugs. She hated craving them. She hated this dumb drug dealer who had gotten her hooked in the first place, and she was terrified of him. She had made her mind up that this was absolutely *the last time!*

"Not a very good, idea," mumbled Nicki. "Just give me the usual stuff, and please hurry. I've got to get back to work."

"I left the coke out in my car. You'll have to wait until I go after it…or you could just take this hit. It's right here, ready for you," sleaze oozed from the mouth of the dealer.

"I'm kickin' this stuff, you hear! This is the last time. After tomorrow morning, it'll all be history, and so will you," cried Nicki. She began to shake, salivating at the thought of getting another hit.

"Where's the money, honey?"

Nicki reached into the low-cut blouse she wore and brought out several bills that had been hidden in her bra. "Here it is. Go get the stuff," she pleaded. "And hurry it up!"

Speaking softly, the dealer took the cap off of the syringe, pushed the air bubbles out of the top, and advanced toward Nicki, saying, "All your pain will be gone in an instant with this tiny prick."

Before Nicki could rise from the chair, the needle was plunged into her carotid artery and injected. She started to scream. The dealer covered her mouth, removed the syringe from her neck and dropped it into a coat pocket.

"This will only take a few seconds, Nicki, my girl, and then all your problems will be over!" Wide-eyed, Nicki grabbed her neck, gurgled in surprise, stiffened, and collapsed back into the chair. She was dead.

***

In Total Darkness

Chapter Five

Tom Howell awoke in his own bed with a rip-roaring headache. He gagged as the taste in his mouth reminded him of the previous evening.

"Hi there! Welcome back to the Land of the Living, Darling," cooed Ginger sweetly. She was sitting in the bedside chair with the morning newspaper in her lap. "I was beginning to think you were going to sleep all day. Can I get you something? Maybe a glass of water?"

"Uh huh. Water," mumbled Tom. "Oh, my head hurts!"

"Dr. Ciccone said the effects of the ipecac were only temporary, and you should be feeling fine as soon as it washes out of your system. The vomiting didn't last long, and the diarrhea and drowsiness should be gone by now. I don't know why you have a headache, though. Dr. Tony didn't mention that as a side effect."

"Would you mind telling me what this "ipecac" thing is all about?" asked Tom.

Ginger answered from the bathroom as she filled a glass with water, "Doc says that you ingested some ipecac. That's the stuff they use to induce vomiting, and boy does it ever work! Did you take it on purpose so you wouldn't have to give the speech, or did you eat or drink something unusual?" She handed him the glass of water.

Tom took a sip of the water, raised one eyebrow and gave his wife a dirty look. He then ran his fingers through his hair, thought for a moment, and remembering, said, "THE COFFEE! It had to be the coffee! I had been sipping it while it was hot, left to go to the men's room, and when I came back I took a big gulp of it before I walked into the ballroom. I remember telling Chuck that it was the nastiest tasting stuff I'd ever had and he needed to pour it out and make a fresh pot."

"Now, how do you suppose ipecac got into your coffee?" asked Ginger.

"I have no idea. Chuck poured me the coffee; I set the cup down on the edge of the bar. When I came out of the men's room, the coffee was right where I left it, and I took a big gulp of it."

"Did you see anyone in the lounge when you were there, or when you came out?"

"The place was full of people. Several walked by and spoke to me. Let's see, I remember speaking to Mike, Dr. Ciccone, Grant and his girlfriend. That new lady, Ava Grissom and her "bodyguard" came by and said hello, and lots of other people. I also saw Nicki, but she didn't come by my table or speak to me," said Tom.

"Of course it might have been some teenager, just playing a prank. You know. Like putting a laxative into chocolate cookies or candy." Ginger paused. "Chalk up another weird thing on your list, Babe! Oh, and by the way, you don't want to forget your meeting with Nicki this morning, so if you're feeling better you might want to hit the shower. I've got to make a mail-run to the office building, plus I have an early tee time today at Four Hills as a guest with the old gang. Then I'll need to get to the carpet store. It's bill-paying day, and I need to be there to sign the checks." With this comment, Ginger walked quickly out the door.

As the hot water pounded his broad shoulders, Tom began to dwell on the events of the previous evening. He hadn't had an opportunity to ask Ginger if she delivered his speech, or what the reaction of the members had been. He began to feel the frustration of not knowing who or why someone was bugging him with this silly nonsense. There didn't seem to be any rhyme or reason for it, other than to annoy him. Drying off and dressing quickly, he began to concentrate on the business of the day. He should be hearing from Nicki sometime this morning. "I wonder what she has in mind," he said aloud.

*

The morning began with the usual routine at Rio Grande Country Club. Janitors began the clean up after the late night dinner-dance, their vacuums humming along with an off-beat rhythm, creating their own special symphony. Downstairs in the ladies' locker room the attendant, Katy, lifted the heavy bucket of ice and dumped it into the thermal box. The effort caused her black face to glisten with droplets of sweat.

"Whew! I'm gettin' too ole for this job," she stated to the empty room. "Guess one o' these days I'm a-gonna haveta think 'bout retirin'." Katy had moved from Four Hills Country Club to Rio Grande Country Club when it opened. It was much closer to her modest south valley home, saving her both time and gasoline money. Many of her "ladies" had also made the move and had begged her to come with them.

Katy put a bowl of fresh-cut lemon wedges in the edge of the ice, placed the two large coffee carafes on the table and proceeded to fill the creamer and sugar containers. She hummed a little hymn as she worked—her mind on the church service she had attended on Sunday night. She replenished the stack of paper cups, straws, and napkins, then stepped back to survey her work. Satisfied, she rolled the service table over to the door leading into the shower room.

The women rarely used the showers, so Katy had decided to use that space to store her service table, brooms, and other cleaning supplies. She pushed the cart through the door and reached for the toilet brush and cleaners. Out of the corner of her eye, she noticed a maroon waitress skirt, and turned to speak. Her words turned into ear-splitting screams as she saw Nicolette du Pree, hanging lifeless from the light fixture attached to the wall.

"AAEEEEEE!" screamed Katy. "Oh, my God, ohmygod, ohmygod, ohmygod!" She turned and ran screaming out of the room, through the lockers, and out into the hallway.

"What on earth!" cried Mike Stevens, coming out of his office. "Whoa, Katy, what's the matter? Are you hurt? Slow down, now, and tell me what's going on?"

Katy's eyes were wild with terror, and wordlessly she pointed at the locker room.

"Okay, okay, okay, now just calm down a bit, and tell me what's wrong," soothed Mike. Other doors had opened and people were gathering around the frightened attendant.

Finally, Katy was able to mouth the words, "In the shower!"

Mike put one of the maids in charge of Katy, then he and a couple of janitors headed into the locker room.

"*Madre de Dios!*" cried one of the janitors, crossing himself.

"What on earth...." said another one.

Mike said nothing as he looked up at the limp body of the woman he loved with all his heart. Her long red hair hung over most of her face, not quite covering the dark green eyes that were wide and staring, no longer sparkling with life. She hung by the shower curtain tieback that had been placed around her chest, under her arms, and over the sconce attached to the wall, the toes of her shoes barely touching the floor. The pert little waitress uniform now made Nicki look like a rag doll, discarded by her mistress. Katy had turned on the light when she entered the room, and now that light shined down on the dark red hair, making it appear to be on fire.

Finally, Mike said flatly, "Don't touch anything. Go call the police. She's not going to need a doctor."

*

Homicide Detective Pete Lucero groaned as he reached over to answer the stark jangling of the telephone by his bedside.

Three hours of sleep simply wasn't enough, he thought, as he glimpsed the 7:30 shining back at him from the digital readout on his clock radio.

Since Carmen had left him and taken the kids, it didn't seem to matter how many sheep he counted, how much he envisioned black velvet, or how many times he played the CD of the ocean sounds, sleep eluded him. He refused to get on the merry-go-round of sleeping pills and amphetamines to keep him going up and down like a carousel horse.

"Lucero," he mumbled into the phone.

"Mornin', Pete. It's Mahoney here," said Patrick, brightly. "We've had a call that there's a dead body at Rio Grande Country Club. A homicide from the sounds of things. Shall I drive by and pick you up?" Patrick Mahoney had been working with Pete for a few years now, and was aware of the sleeping situation since Carmen left. "I'll pick up a sausage and egg biscuit for you on the way. Do you want orange juice or coffee?"

Pete had come alive at the words "dead body" and was hurriedly heading for the shower. "Coffee, you dumb jerk, you know that! About a gallon of it!" He knew Patrick would not take offense at the comment. "Fifteen minutes. Pick me up in fifteen minutes."

Things had been pretty busy for the Homicide Division for several months. Pete let hot water scald him awake as he remembered the killer that had been strangling women and cutting off their heads; then the series of drug-related murders between gang members; and now this. "It's no wonder Carmen left me," he said into the towel as he dried himself. Quickly he jerked on his clothes, noticing how loose they had become. "No woman in her right mind would put up with this crap!" Running the comb through his dark wavy hair, he noticed a gray one that had appeared at his temple, the first one he had seen. He wasn't prepared for how much that one gray hair disturbed him. "Damn! That's all I need." He grabbed his coat and waited for Patrick as the car pulled up to his front door.

"All set, partner?" asked Mahoney as he handed him the sack from McDonald's.

"Set. Roll 'em," said Pete. He pulled out a cigarette and started to light it, paused and looked at Patrick, frowned, and stuck the unlit cigarette back into his pocket.

Patrick Mahoney was a real model of the Irish policeman. He was six-feet-two inches tall, a lean and muscled two hundred fifteen pounds, had a strawberry blond crew-cut and blue eyes. A few freckles had the audacity to sprinkle themselves across his nose. He excelled with the computer, passed the test to become a detective with ease, and had requested assignment with Pete Lucero.

"How are the Spanish lessons coming along?" asked Pete as they sped toward the country club.

"Very slowly, *mi amigo,* very slowly" responded Patrick.

Mahoney and Lucero pulled up in front of Rio Grande Country Club just in front of the team from the Unit for Forensic Investigation.

At first glance, Pete didn't see any particular "cause of death". He turned to Patrick and said, "What's your take on this, Pat? There is no blood or evidence of trauma that is visible."

"Hard to say. It might take autopsy to figure this one out. We'll ask for a priority rush on it from the lab," replied his partner. Neither of the detectives noticed the tiny puncture wound on her neck, covered by her long red hair.

"We need to talk to the manager of the club here, maybe get a list of employees to talk to, and see what shakes out," decided Pete.

"I'm on it." said Patrick quickly heading out of the locker room toward the bank of offices lining the hallway.

It didn't take Patrick long to come back with a list of employees of Rio Grande Country Club. He had circled some names on the list.

"So, what's with the circles, Pat?" Pete asked his partner.

"Well, the body is Nicolette du Pree, a waitress. This Paula," said Pat as he pointed to a name on the list, "is another waitress, and worked the same shift with Nicki. She had quite a lot to say, even though she was pretty shook up. Nicki was a busy little gal. Paula gave me at least three names of men that Nicki either lived with or had an affair with. Two of them were married at the time."

"Go on," requested Pete.

"The first man was Bud Simpson. Cowboy-type transplanted Texan. Brags a lot about his Daddy's oilfields down around Houston, and uses his money to entice pretty young girls to be "nice" to him. His wife, Claire, hasn't a clue that he is misbehaving, and from what they say, his "business-trips" are usually made in his forty-foot long motor home, complete with all the amenities. Paula says that he started in on Nicki the very first day she came to work. Brought her gifts, showered her with attention, that sort of thing. Guess he really made her angry one night, and she gave him a black eye."

"Hmm. Wonder how he made her so angry? And would a black eye give him a reason to get even?"

"Possible. I'd bet he's pretty macho from the sounds of things. Wouldn't take too kindly to being put in his place by a babe."

"Ok, who is next?" asked Pete.

"You have already met the next one," replied Patrick, consulting his notebook. "Mike Stevens, the assistant club manager. He was there when the body was first discovered. Paula said he was so smitten by Nicki that he left his wife and children, moved in with Nicki and was ready to marry her and adopt her little boy."

"By the way, where is that little boy? Did you ask anyone about him?" asked Pete.

"Paula said that a babysitter named Bertha would keep him until next of kin could be reached. She has been with him since he was born. Came with Nicki from Florida. The little boy is named "Trey". That usually means there is a father named the same with a Roman numeral II behind it. Ex-husbands are usually on the suspect list.

"So then what about Mike Stevens?"

"I guess Nicki tossed him out on his ear, and the next day a Dr. Antonio Ciccone moved into her house. This is all secondhand rumors, but is easily checked," replied Patrick. Paula said that Mike Stevens had really fallen hard and was devastated when Nicki kicked him out. He had destroyed his family for her and was now out in the cold."

"Definite suspect! Now what about this Dr. Coconut?"

"Ciccone. Chuh-cone-ee. Single. Looks like Kenny Rogers. Silver hair, full beard, mustache, manicured hands, deep bass voice, and loves the ladies. They love him, too. One of the most eligible bachelors in town. Paula was pretty surprised that he would consent to moving in with anyone, as that would be too much of a commitment."

"Womanizer. Probably very vain. Wonder if Nicki booted him as well? Is he still at her house? Wounded pride would definitely make him a suspect."

***

Chapter Six

Ginger Howell was about sixty yards from the eighteenth green at Four Hills Country Club. She mindlessly reached into her golf bag and pulled out a wedge, took a practice swing, lined up the ball, and promptly shanked it into the greenside bunker.

"Good grief," she moaned.

"What was *that* all about?" asked Jean, her playing partner for the day.

"I haven't a clue," answered Ginger. "My mind certainly isn't on golf this morning, that's for sure."

"All gifts are certainly appreciated," laughed Dotti, one of the opponents of the day.

"Yeah, that means you have to chip in from the bunker, just to tie," exclaimed Rosalie.

The four women finished the round, had the bag boys take their clubs for storage, and went into the locker room to wash up. They were still talking about Ginger's missed shot on the last hole on the way up the stairs to the lounge. It was standard procedure to have a soft drink following the round while settling up the small bets. "It isn't the *amount* of the wager that matters, but just *who* gets to hold the quarters," was a common statement among the women.

The lounge had glass windows on three sides, so the members could look out over the golf course while they relaxed with meals or drinks. Since it was now September, the course was in excellent condition. The fairway grass was like velvet, the greens were recovering from the heavy number of players during the summer, and the fall aeration and sanding wasn't due for another couple of weeks. The course was well established, having been built in the late 50's, and was a traditional style golf course lined with houses around the perimeter. The tall cottonwood, sycamore, and ash trees were complimented by the flowering ornamentals, and all the planting areas were rife with a profusion of flowers for color. As Four Hills was located in the Manzano Mountain foothills, there was an unobstructed view of the city's west side, as well as a panoramic view of majestic Mount Taylor on the western horizon at least sixty miles away.

Another foursome of ladies joined the four women in the lounge, and the atmosphere was cordial and relaxed as the women figured out the winnings for the game of the day, sipped their soft drinks, and enjoyed the spectacular view.
"I apologize, Jean. I have so many other things running through my mind, it's a wonder that I found my way back to the clubhouse." said Ginger.
"Well, today's game certainly didn't live up to your potential, so what gives?" asked Jean.
"I guess it's that darned office building." moaned Ginger. "I didn't realize just how much it was weighing on my mind. Since the partnership broke up we haven't had time to hire someone to take care of distributing mail and some of the problems that a full-time manager would handle. Tom and I have been taking turns trying to keep things running smoothly at the building while we look for a manager. And we also need to keep business running as usual at Howell Carpets."
"What office building are you talking about, Gin?" asked Rosalie.
"Well, it's quite a long story, but the history of the building is really rather interesting. Are you sure you really want to know?" asked Ginger.

"C'mon, Gin, give," said Jean.

Ginger sighed and then began the story. "Tom and I became co-owners of the 16,000 square foot office building just off Lomas at Wyoming when the owner of one of the largest house-moving companies in the state approached us about a financial interest in a venture he was undertaking. Roger Williams had just signed a contract with the Federal Government to clear the office buildings off of the newly closed Air Force base at Amarillo, Texas."

"Clear them off? What did he do with the buildings?" asked Dotti.

"Several of the buildings have already been moved and turned into homes. The buildings were all thirty feet wide by sixty feet long and were two-story. Roger had figured out how to cut two holes in either end of the sixty-foot lengths, insert huge steel beams down the entire length of the building, and then cut the buildings in half horizontally."

"How do you cut a building in half?" asked Rosalie.

"With some sort of masonry saw, I suppose. Anyway, at this point, he used tall heavy-duty jacks and literally "jacked up" the beams, lifting the second floor off of the first floor. Then the crew tore out the first floor of the building, reserving all of the usable lumber and any other salvageable construction materials.

"Wow! I'll bet that was really something to see," commented Diane.

"No kidding," echoed Jean.

"Anyway, after they cleared out the debris, a couple of dollies were pulled beneath the building and the jacks were lowered until the steel beams rested on the dollies." As Ginger spoke, she used her hands to illustrate what she was describing. "Then they simply hitched the dollies to a tractor rig to be towed to whatever destination. It really is quite a sight to see a building of this size moving down the interstate. Williams used four of these buildings to construct an office building in the form of a quadrangle, with a forty-foot square interior atrium inside."

"Sounds like a pretty intricate process," stated Diane. "How did it work out?"

"Well, after moving each building to Albuquerque, the beams under the original second story were once more jacked up, a new first floor was constructed on a cement slab, and then the second story was lowered onto the top of the first floor. It was very imaginative construction, which baffled the city construction inspectors no end. They couldn't find anything wrong with it, however, and they green tagged it."

"Once the four wings were completed, entryways were created on the north and south sides of the building, and additional office space was framed in on the second floor above the entryways. Stairways were built on all four sides of the building to be used as fire escapes. Solar panels were installed over the interior atrium, making the planting space a virtual "greenhouse" for plants. Inside, stairs were built on either end of the building adjacent to the entryways, leading to a balcony from which one could access any of the offices on the second floor. Roger personally welded circles of steel into an intricate pattern for the railing around the balcony. He also installed some laminated wooden beams that were salvaged out of a church. The over-all effect is outstandingly beautiful. Ficus trees, Norwood pines, dracaena, schefflera, and philodendrons make the atmosphere of the interior building like a garden."

"We've got to go see this building," enthused Rosalie.

Ginger continued the story. "The Williams moved into the building and operated their business as well as managing the office building from that location at first. But, after several months, it was decided to split up, and we took the office building while the Williams took several apartment buildings that had become assets of the partnership. After the split, the Williams moved out, leaving the building without a manager. So that about brings you up to date," said Ginger.

"Amazing. That must have really been something to see those buildings moving down the highway," exclaimed Rosalie.

"What did they do about underpasses and things like that?" asked Dotti.

"Well, they had to plot a course around all of them, of course, as well as any utility lines and the likes once they came into town," answered Ginger. "And one more interesting thing...I had a phone call this morning from our mysterious lady stranger, you know, the one with the bodyguard that was at the meeting the other night? It seems that she is interested in leasing some office space."

"Are you talking about Ava Grissom?" asked Dotti.

"That's right," replied Ginger. I can't wait to talk with her."

Diane's cell phone rang about that time. She answered the call and then said, "What? When did it happen? Do they know who did it?"

All the women waited to hear what had happened, as all the color had drained from Diane's face as she had listened. She then turned to the women and said, "Katy found the body of one of the waitresses at Rio Grande this morning. They think she was murdered!"

***

Chapter Seven

At Howell Carpets, Tom had spent the morning going over quarterly sales reports. In the back of his mind, he kept wondering about Nicki du Pree, and why she hadn't called him. When Nancy buzzed him that Grant McGuire was on the phone for him, it broke his concentration.

"Yo, Grant," Tom answered the phone. "What's up?"

"Did you hear the news about Nicki du Pree?" asked Grant. He was always delighted to be the first one to spread bad news.

"Nicki? No. What news?" asked Tom.

"She was murdered. Sometime last night. They found her body in the ladies locker room this morning. It's all over town by now," said Grant.

"Murdered? Good Lord! I spoke to her on the phone only last night, before the meeting. She was really upset! Do they know who killed her?"

"Not to my knowledge. What did you talk to her on the phone about, if you don't mind my asking?" Grant's voice was constricted, as he tried to sound casual rather than nosy.

"Grant, it was good of you to call me, I have another call coming in now that I have to take. Talk to you later." Tom abruptly hung up the phone. He didn't have another call, but did not want to discuss Nicki with Grant even though he was an old friend. He was certain Grant had put a move on Nicki right after she came to work at the club, and that might possibly have been why she wanted to talk. Anyway, Grant had been acting rather peculiar lately, and since Nicki had mentioned that it might be dangerous, sharing anything with Grant didn't seem proper at this moment.

With his mind still whirling about Nicki's death, Tom was startled when Cherry, the head bookkeeper ran into his office almost in hysterics.

"The whole blamed system is down, Mr. Howell. I can't get into any of my programs!" cried Cherry.

"Whoa, slow down, now what's wrong?"

"My computers. The whole system is down!"

"Cherry, calm down. We have complete backups for all the programs. Just go call the computer tech you usually call, have him re-format and re-load all of the programs. Then your backups will put you back into sync. If he can't come right away, maybe Doc Chapman from Four Hills could help us out."

"Well," said Cherry, calming down some, "the only thing is that we will have to re-input all of the sales data for the past three days."

"How much overtime will that take, Cherry, to bring you current?"

"If I can get the tech out here pretty quickly, we can start as soon as he is finished, then I guess about twelve-fifteen hours to re-input the data."

"Ask the technician if he can determine what caused the crash, Cherry. If he can tell us that, maybe we can prevent it from happening again. And, the overtime is approved, so get cracking."

"Yes, sir, Mr. Howell." Cherry left in a much better mood, anticipating the extra money in her paycheck.

Cherry almost bumped into Ginger Howell as she turned to walk out of Tom's office.

"Oops, sorry, Ginger, didn't look before I leaped," said Cherry, scooting by in a hurry.

"From the look on your face, I can tell that you heard the news about Nicki," said Tom to his wife.

"Yes, Diane got a call while we were settling up in the lounge. Oh, Tom, now we'll never know what she wanted to talk to you about! When she said it was dangerous, she really meant it, didn't she?"

"I just heard the news a few minutes ago. Grant called me, and said it was all over town by now. He was only too happy to pass on the bad news. I didn't say anything to him about Nicki's call, other than I had talked to her on the phone last night and that she was upset. I was just thinking about calling Pete Lucero. Do you have his phone number in that photographic memory of yours?"

"It's been a few months since we talked to him last, but I still remember it," said Ginger. "Here, I'll dial it for you." She picked up the phone and dialed the homicide detective's office from memory.

"Homicide, this is Lucero," he answered.

"Pete, Tom Howell here. Ginger and I just found out about Nicolette du Pree. It may not mean anything at all, but I got a call from her early last night, before we left to go to the meeting at Rio Grande. She seemed very upset, and wanted to make arrangements for a private meeting. When I asked her if she was going to be at the dinner-dance, she said that it would be too dangerous for us to meet then. She used the word *dangerous*. Then the only other thing she mentioned was that she had overheard a conversation that she wasn't supposed to have heard."

"Too bad that she didn't get a chance to tell you what was on her mind," said Pete.

"That's what I thought, too," responded Tom. "If someone hadn't laced my coffee with ipecac, I might have been able to speak to her after my speech, but that really did a number on me, otherwise, I might have been able to corner her sometime during the evening."

"Ipecac? The stuff to make you throw up? Who would do a thing like that?"

"I really don't have a clue, but whoever it was I'd like to knock his jock off—to use an old football saying!" Tom paused, "I know this isn't much, but it does tell you Nicki's frame of mind at the beginning of the evening."

"Thanks for the information, Tom. If you hear anything else don't hesitate to call."

Tom turned to his wife and said, "You heard what Cherry had to say about the computers, didn't you, Ginger?" asked Tom.

"No. She just about ran me over, but I didn't hear what you two were discussing."

"The computers crashed. You may not have to sign checks today after all," reported Tom.

"Well, isn't that a fine kettle of fish! Another annoying incident in the lives of the Howell family." Ginger stopped, remembering the murder. "Nicki would like to be annoyed right now, rather than where she is, I'm sure. Poor girl."

***

Chapter Eight

Ginger picked up the phone and called the number left by Ava Grissom. As she dialed she had a mental image of the woman dressed in her gold and silver silk outfit, sitting by her rough-looking companion.

"Hello, Ms. Grissom, this is Ginger Howell. My schedule has changed a bit, and I will be able to meet you at the office building to show you that space if you have time."

"That's great," responded Ava. "I can meet you there in fifteen minutes, if that is all right?"

"Perfect," replied Ginger. "I'll see you there."

Ava had made up quite an elaborate story to tell her sister-in-law about why she left Houston in such as hurry. Telling stories was one of her real strong points. She glanced around at the modest home and realized that she had to work fast to find an office and another place to stay before her ex-husband found out that she had temporarily moved in with his sister.

Ava quickly slipped on the velvet sweat pants and top that looked much more expensive than they were, swept her blond hair into an up-do, and quickly refreshed her make-up and eye shadow. Then she put on all of the cubic zirconium rings that looked so much like real diamonds. She would have to borrow a car from the next-door neighbor, but that shouldn't be a problem. The sweet old lady next door had been very helpful and would always respond to whatever "emergency" thought up for the moment.

"What else do I need? Image is everything," she reminded herself, taking a quick peek in the full length mirror on her closet door. Satisfied, she left in a hurry in order to park the old car and be waiting in the building, so that Ginger Howell would not see what she was driving. No one needed to know that her husband had kicked her out of the house in Houston and filed for divorce immediately after finding out that she had been arrested for fraud. She had managed to beat the indictment, but had not been able to arrange for another vehicle yet. She had called on some old acquaintances to help her get started in another location.

Ginger loved the atrium in the building. It always pleased her to smell the green plants that were so happily growing beneath the solar panels. It never ceased to amaze her to see ficus trees that had to be pruned to keep them from growing through the solar panels that were two stories high, and the philodendrons covering the ground below. It was a moment before she realized that a woman was standing by the reader board, reading the listing of all the tenants in the building. It was Ava.

"Ava Grissom? I'm Ginger Howell. So pleased to meet you." Ginger warmly shook the hand extended to her. "The suite of offices that is available is on the second floor, up in the southeast corner of the building. If you'll follow me, I'll show you the way."

Ginger dug the master key out of her purse as the two women ascended the stairs to the second floor, and opened the door into the empty suite. "There are about fifteen hundred square feet total, with a corner executive office, a reception area, a secondary office—for an assistant or the like, and a small room for kitchen area and office machines. The lease is for a year, with first and last month's rent and a security deposit that's due before moving in, you know, the standard stuff."

Ava moved through the offices with a thoughtful expression, as if she was mentally arranging furniture, and then announced, "It's perfect. When can I move in?"

A little surprised, Ginger said, "Well, the space is available now, as you can see. All I need to do is to type up the lease, collect the rent, and give you a key. I do have a few questions first. What is the nature of your business?"

"Oh! I am the American loan agent for the Saudi Arabian Bank of Belgium. I arrange commercial loans for customers using arbitrage profits." The words slid off her tongue as if she had said them hundreds of times.

"That sounds very interesting," replied Ginger. *What the heck is an "arbitrage", anyway?* Aloud she said, "Don't you want to know the amount of the lease, and the monthly payment?"

"It really doesn't matter. The bank has given me carte blanche in setting up this office, so all that really matters is that I *like* it!" Ava, waltzed through the office space again, and smiling at Ginger, said, "I would like to show the space to my companion, Alfred Benedetti. Do you think we could arrange it?"

"Well, certainly," replied Ginger, a bit surprised by the immediate acceptance of the space. It usually took several days for people to make up their minds, gain clearance, and go through channels to take the offices. "What do you have in mind, time-wise?"

"The sooner, the better for me. Could you come back this evening, say about nine o'clock?"

Ginger hesitated. "That's not going to work for me. How about tomorrow?"

Ava frowned her disappointment. "I did want so much to show it to Alfred tonight." She paused, and then said, "What if I borrowed a key to the suite, just so I could show it tonight, then we can sign all of the papers as soon as you have them prepared. How does that sound?"

"I don't know…that's really against our usual policy—but I guess it would be all right. After all, the lease shouldn't take that long to prepare. I will need the legal name to go on the lease, the address of the company responsible for the payment, that sort of thing."

"Here is my business card. It is a temporary one, as I didn't want to have new ones made up until I had a permanent address, but all the information you need is right there." Ava handed her a card. It had quite apparently been printed on a home computer, was slightly smeared, but had the name Saudi Arabian Bank of Belgium printed prominently on it, with Ava Grissom's name as American Representative. The address on the card was an overseas address.

"Don't they have an office in the States?" asked Ginger.

"That's what I am doing here. Setting up the office for the entire nation, right here in Albuquerque."

This was all just a bit much for Ginger. "You know, I think you should meet my husband. Why don't you plan for us to take you out to dinner at Rio Grande Country Club? I am aware that you are a new member there, but please allow us the privilege of welcoming you. Would tomorrow night work?"

"That's perfect. I'll just meet you at the club. It won't be necessary for you to pick me up, as I have a meeting there tomorrow afternoon, anyway. Do you mind eating early?"

"Oh, early is fine. Matter of fact it will work out much better that way. How does six o'clock sound?"

"Six o'clock would be a good time for me."

"Six it is, then. I'll have to go to my office here in the building and get you a key to the suite. I only have the master key with me, and since it opens all of the offices in the building it's one that I have to keep in my possession."

"Fine. I'd like to spend some more time here thinking about furniture arrangement, if you don't mind."

Ginger hesitated, but then agreed. "I'm a bit hesitant, as I usually give tenants a sort of "building orientation" when they sign the lease, but I guess that it will be okay, since the papers will be ready to sign by tomorrow."

"Thank you so much. I won't be too long," said Ava enthusiastically.

"You'll have to go before the last tenant in the building leaves. That way they can lock the outer doors and set the alarm system."

"Of course, I understand completely. I'll be sure to check that I can see lights on in some of the other offices and I'll also check the parking lot to make sure there are cars still here."

After Ginger had given her the key and left the building, Ava quickly dialed Alfred Benedetti on her cell phone.

"Al, it's me. I have office space! Get over here right away. We have our work cut out for us. We'll need phones, desks and chairs, office equipment, paper and supplies, a coffee machine, and we'll need to find someone who can type and answer the telephone!" Ava was excited.

"That sounds good. When will you get possession?"

"I have the key to the suite of offices now. The owner is going to type up a lease and have it ready for me to sign by tomorrow. Isn't it awesome?"

"Not too bad."

"How soon can you get over here?"

"Whoa! Are you calling from the office now?"

"Yes."

"Is the office furnished?"

"No."

"Then you don't have a telephone book, a place to sit, or anything to write on? And are you calling me on your sister-in-law's cell phone?"

"No, I borrowed the old lady's car that lives next door, and also her cell phone."

"I'm not sure it's a good idea to set all this up from an empty office. Why don't you meet me where we can sit down, get organized, and do this properly," suggested Al.

"You are right, of course, and I need to get this car back to the neighbor. We've got to do something about a vehicle, too, right away!"

"We can use my old car until you have a chance to buy a new one. I'll meet you at your house in fifteen minutes," said Al, as he hung up the phone.

Alfred Benedetti shook his head in frustration. *"This dame just may not be worth the trouble, simply to have a good cover-up,"* he said to himself. When his boss had asked him to work with Ava as a "bodyguard" he had not realized what a ditzy little lady he would be stuck with for hours at a time. It never paid for him to argue with the Boss, though, and he wasn't about to start now—especially with the kind of money he had been offered. Al sighed and picked up his car keys. "I guess I can handle any dame for a short period of time. I just hope that the Boss gets everything settled quickly so I can dump this old broad!"

***

Chapter Nine

Homicide Detective Pete Lucero shuffled the stack of papers on his desk and made piles of the different reports that cluttered the desktop. "Okay, Pat, let's recap the info that we've got."

"Okay, partner, here's what's on my list so far. First, I interrogated all the rest of the employees at the club. The only one that knew anything at all about Nicolette du Pree's personal life was Paula, the waitress that worked the same shift—and we had already talked with her. It seems Nicki didn't fraternize with the employees, except for the assistant club manager, Mike Stevens. I want to talk with him in more detail as I think he might be considered a suspect," said Patrick.

"Matter of fact, I think you need to have that Stevens guy, that Texan, and Dr. Coconut all come talk to us. We'll start with those three," said Pete.

Patrick made a note. "I also was able to run down Nicolette du Pree's married name by checking the computer for marriage licenses. They are public record, as you are aware. Nicki was married three times. She was very young when she married Robert O'Grady, divorced him two years later, and immediately married Richard Harrigan, who was old enough to be her father. There were newspaper articles about their wedding, as Harrigan was filthy rich. He died when they had been married only a short time, and left his fortune to Nicki. She didn't mourn him very long, as she married the third time to a man named Michael Cadrigan within a few months. He is Trey's father."

"Wow, that's quite a track record. Millionaire widow becomes cocktail waitress? Did you find any info in your computer about what happened in between?"

"Cadrigan's name came up several times in the newspaper search I ran on him. Most of the articles were about real estate deals that went south, and then most recently he declared bankruptcy, so we know all of the money is gone, unless Nicki has some hidden away somewhere. I also checked to see if he had a record. There were several DUI's and an arrest for drug violation—cocaine, I think."

"Looks like poor Nicki had some bad luck in the husband department. What can you find out about the first husband? Would he be a suspect in her murder?"

"I did a search on him, too. He still lives in the East, has married again, and birth records show him with three children. He works for the post office in their old hometown. Seems to be pretty stable."

"Yeah, I don't think we'll need to worry about him, especially since she had been married twice since then. And he seems to be happily remarried himself."

"That's what I was thinking, too."

"Were you able to trace this Cadrigan guy?"

"As I said, he had been arrested for DUI, charged with possession of cocaine, got out on bail, then apparently OD'ed. He was buried three months ago, so it looks like we can wipe the slate clean on her past."

"Sounds like we'd better concentrate on the "present" instead of her past, huh?"

"I think so," replied Patrick

"Oh yeah—what's the status on finding "next-of-kin" for Trey? If Nicki's parents or siblings are still alive they might be interested in custody of the little boy. Were you able to track them down?"

"Still working on that. We have her hometown, and her birth record, so it shouldn't be too hard to find them."

Just then an officer came into the room and handed the detectives an autopsy report. Pete quickly read through the report and silently handed it to Patrick.

Patrick started reading it aloud. "Blood work showed traces of cocaine, caffeine, nicotine, and *sodium pentobarbital*? Good grief! That's the chemical that veterinarians use for animal euthanasia!" he cried.

"Somebody had her put to sleep—like an animal? Did they give her a shot, like a dog? Or how did they give it to her?" Pete was astounded.

"The coroner found a puncture wound in her carotid artery. Death would have been almost instantaneous, as the chemical would have gone directly into her brain," said Patrick.

"So who has access to sodium pentobarbital?"

"Vets, of course, pharmacies, how about medical doctors, as in *Dr.Ciccone?*"

Pete became agitated. "Pat, old buddy, this is right up your alley. Want to see what you can find out from the sources? I'll go to work on the other leads that we have. Oh, and you might see if your handy-dandy computer can find Trey's grandparents."

"That should be easy enough to do." He paused. "We also know that Nicki had cocaine in her system. Where do you suppose she got it? Do we have any informants that could help with that?"

"Hmm. I wonder if Ricky the Rat is still around. Maybe I'll try to contact him."

"I will request that Stevens, Simpson, and Ciccone come down to the station. If all of them agree to come, we won't have to pick them up," said Patrick.

"Do you still have Ricky's number in your rolodex?"

Mike Stevens blinked, sighed, and then asked the receptionist for Pete Lucero's office. He had no feeling.

Numb. It was if someone had extinguished his life source fire. His Nicki was dead.

"Have a seat, Mr. Stevens," said Pete Lucero. "I have a few questions for you."

Mike woodenly sat down in the chair in front of Pete's desk, straight as a rod. He didn't say anything.

"How long did you know Nicolette du Pree?"

"Thirteen months."

"And when did you first meet her?"

"The day she walked into Rio Grande Country Club to apply for a job."

"She interviewed with you, and you hired her?"

"On the spot."

"How would you characterize your relationship with Ms. du Pree?"

"I loved her."

"It is common knowledge that you left your wife and family and moved in with Ms. du Pree, is that correct?"

"Yes."

Pete looked up at Patrick, with a question in his eyes. Patrick shrugged his shoulders.

"Mr. Stevens, we need to find whoever killed Nicolette du Pree. Can you help us at all?"

"No."

"I am going to need more than yes or no from you, Mr. Stevens. Tell us what you were doing all evening the night Nicolette was killed."

Mike's shoulders slumped, he took a deep breath and looked around, and seemed to awaken from the stupor he was in. "I spent the early part of the evening checking to make sure everything was ready for the meeting, the dinner, and the dance. I made sure the PA system was working properly; that all of the wait staff were present and doing their preparations as they should. Nicki was doing exactly what she should be doing, setting napkins and silverware on the dining tables. She looked beautiful, as she always did. I noticed that she was laughing and talking with Paula, but after a while she seemed tense, rather nervous, as if something had upset her. I asked her if everything was all right. She simply smiled at me and nodded her head."

"This was before the meeting began?"

"Yes. I spoke to several of the members, and then went up to the podium to introduce Tom Howell, who was to give the *President's Outlook* speech."

"Did you happen to notice Ms. du Pree after that?"

"Well, there was a lot of excitement when Mr. Howell got violently ill. His wife had to give his speech. Then the dinner seemed to go off without a hitch. I was watching all of the wait staff to make sure the food was served properly. Nicki took care of her station with no problems. She was supposed to have a break at nine o'clock. I saw her going down the back stairs about that time. She liked to smoke those little brown cigarillos."

"And after that?"

Mike's face went white; he swallowed hard, and blinked several times to keep the tears from forming in his eyes. "The next time I saw Nicki was in the shower when Katy came screaming out of the ladies locker room the next morning." Mike's voice cracked. "I knew by looking at Nicki's eyes that she was dead. They were totally lifeless."

"I know this is hard for you. It's quite apparent that you cared deeply for Nicki," said Patrick. "Are you familiar with a solution called sodium pentobarbital?" he asked.

"No, what is it?" asked Mike.

"Were you aware that Nicki was using cocaine?" asked Pete, ignoring the question.

"Yes. I could tell that she was taking something. I didn't know that it was cocaine, for sure."

"Got any idea about where she was getting it?"

"No. Maybe from Dr. Ciccone," Mike said with venom.

"You don't care for Dr. Ciccone, I take it," said Patrick.

"When Nicki asked me to leave, the good doctor moved right into her house. I had destroyed my family, and now he was taking Nicki away from me....no, I *don't care for Dr. Ciccone!*" said Mike vehemently. "I loved Nicki with every fiber of my being. It was torture to see her at work every day, knowing that she was sleeping with him!" Now he was seething with anger.

"Okay, Mr. Stevens, we don't have any more questions for you right now, but stay available."

After Mike left his office, Patrick asked Pete, "What's your gut feeling about this guy?"

"I think that he really, really loved Nicki. But with that kind of intensity, jealousy becomes a pretty strong motive, you know, "if I can't have her then no one else can have her either" syndrome. I think we need to keep Mike Stevens on our list."

*

Antonio Ciccone smiled at his patient, while soothing her with his deep bass voice. She gazed adoringly at him as he took her by the elbow and ushered her out of his office.

"Now, don't you worry about a thing. We'll take care of you. Just tell the receptionist to schedule you for another appointment as soon as possible after next Tuesday. We should have the results back from the tests by then." As soon as the woman was gone, Dr. Ciccone turned back into his office, muttering to himself, "You old bat! There's not a thing wrong with you."

He had taken the rest of the day off to play in the Labor Day golf tournament at Rio Grande Country Club, but when the detectives contacted him, he arranged to meet with them after his last appointment but before his tee time, hoping that they wouldn't keep him too long.

He ran a brush through his silver gray hair, cleaned his polished fingernails, took a swig of mouthwash to clean his breath, gave his image in the mirror a critical eye, and liked what he saw. He didn't need to impress the detectives, but one never knew what kind of pretty little thing might be sitting at the front desk. He then quickly shed his white coat and reached for his jacket. He was apprehensive about the meeting with Lucero, but was really looking forward to the afternoon round of golf in the gorgeous September weather.

He pushed the button for the intercom, and said to his receptionist, "I won't be in for the rest of the afternoon. Do *not* beep me unless it is a dire emergency. Dr. DeCostner will be covering for me, so you can call him if necessary."

*

To his chagrin, the receptionist at the police station was overweight, middle-aged, wore thick glasses, and had mousy brown hair. When she spoke, however, it was the voice of an angel.

"Detective Lucero would like for you to go right on back to his office, Dr. Ciccone," the silky voice told him.

"Have a seat, Dr. Ciccone," offered Pete. "I'm sure you know why you are here."

"Nicolette du Pree, of course," said the doctor, his deep voice resonating in the small office.

"We know you had moved in with Nicki. Are you still living at her house?"

"As a matter of fact, I am not. I moved back into my own house the end of last week."

"And what were the circumstances that prompted the move," queried Patrick.

"It was by mutual agreement. I think that both of us were used to having more…*variety,* in our lives." He gave the detectives a knowing look.

Patrick actually blushed.

Pete frowned, and said, "Please elaborate, doctor."

"Well," said the doctor, leaning forward and speaking in a confidential tone of voice, "I don't think it is any secret that

Nicolette has had many lovers, and as a matter of fact, so have I. I have never moved in with any of them before, however, and I wouldn't have moved in with Nicki, but I thought she had a really special quality."

"So you both decided that it wasn't working out?"

"That's right."

"How long had you been living with her?"

"It was just over three months, right after the first of June."

Pete changed the subject. "Where were you between eight forty-five and nine thirty the night she was killed?"

"I am not certain, but I think that I was on the dance floor. I danced with several different women during the evening, but Paula might remember the names. I think she keeps an eye on me."

Patrick was writing all of this information in his notebook. Without looking up he asked, "Doctor, do you use recreational drugs?"

"Absolutely not! I prescribe drugs all the time. When patients have to have pain killers for an extended length of time, I am aware of what it can do to them—the dangers of addiction. I have way too much pride to let myself become an addict, with no control over my life. I've seen drugs destroy too many people," he stated emphatically.

"You are aware that Nicki was using cocaine?"

"I wasn't at first. But yes, I became aware of it. That's another part of the reason I moved out."

"Okay, other than variety and cocaine, what is the rest of the reason?"

"I had reason to believe that Nicki had taken another lover, behind my back."

"Were you jealous of her?"

"Disappointed, yes. Jealous, no."

"Doctor, do you have access to sodium pentobarbital?"

A strange look came upon Dr. Ciccone's face. "Sodium pentobarbital? Yes, I suppose that I could get it if necessary." He frowned, his mind racing ahead to anticipate the next question.

"Nicki was killed by an injection of it. She died instantly."

"And you think that I injected her with it?"

"We didn't say that doctor. We are just exploring all the possibilities," answered Pete.

"Who else can you think of that might have access to such a solution?" asked Patrick.

"Well, I guess any doctor could write a prescription for it, a pharmacist of course, a veterinarian, drug company employees or representatives, possibly others," he replied.

"Thank you for your cooperation doctor. We may need to talk with you again, so please don't plan any out of town trips without contacting us first," stated Pete, as he stood up to indicate that the meeting was finished. Dr. Ciccone rose and left without another word.

*

"Possibility?" asked Pete.

"Definite possibility," replied Patrick, writing in his notebook. "I'll call the front desk to see if Bud Simpson is here. Are you ready for him?"

"Yeah, I guess so. We don't seem to be eliminating anyone at this point." The angel's voice in the intercom announced that Bud Simpson was waiting.

As Bud Simpson entered Pete's office, he took off his cowboy hat and held it in front of him, twirling it nervously.

"Mr. Simpson, have a seat. We'd like to ask you a few questions regarding your relationship with Nicolette du Pree," said Pete.

"What would you like to know," asked Bud, as he plopped down in the chair. "I was really shocked to learn she had been killed. She was such a pretty little thing."

"Were you at Rio Grande County Club Monday evening?" asked Patrick.

"Oh, sure. Claire and I love to dance. We never miss an opportunity." His Texas drawl made it sound like "opp-or-toon-i-tee".

"Did you stay for the entire evening?"

"Yep. Claire and I were never apart, 'cept when she went to th' ladies room. She was gone, oh, 'bout ten minutes, and we didn't miss a single dance. We love that country music they were playing."

"We were told that you had an affair with Nicki. Is that correct?"

Bud put on a slow smile. "Yep. She was *such* a pretty lil' thing. I just couldn't resist those big ol' green eyes. Whew! And she was some kind of woman, too. Guess she got tired of me, or I'd still be hangin' around her," he stopped, remembering that she was dead. "What a waste."

"Mr. Simpson, is your wife aware of the affair that you had with Nicki?"

"NO! And please don't tell her! I love Claire with all my heart and I don't want to hurt her even one little bit. It's just that I've got this itch I have to scratch ever once in a while, if you know what I mean," said Bud with a wink.

"Did you know that Nicki was using cocaine?"

"Well, yeah, she was just beginnin' to dabble in it when we were sleepin' t'gether...but I didn't use it with her," he avowed.

"Do you know where she got it?"

"Nope. I think she was sleeping with another guy about the same time. Tall fellow, salt and pepper hair. Mighta got it from him."

"Do you know his name?"

"See him a lot, around the club, but don't know who he is. But if I see him again, I'll ask around and find out his name."

"We would appreciate a call if you happen to find out who he is."

"Mr. Simpson, do you have cows or horses on your property?"

"Sure! Lots o' cows, handful of horses. It reminds me of Texas, even though we live in New Mexico now."

"Have you ever had to "put down" an animal?"

"Lots of times. Had this one cow, stepped in a gopher hole and broke her leg, dab nigh clear in two. Critter was hurtin' fearful-like. I didn't have my guns over here then, so I called the vet, and he gave her a shot, put her right to sleep."

"Did the vet leave any more shots like that with you, just in case it ever happened again?"

"I didn't check the barn, but I don't think so. I'm sure he woulda said sumpthin' if he had. What's that got to do with Nicki?"

"Did Nicki ever threaten to tell your wife about your affair?"

"Well, she got mad one night, when I started joking about her little boy being named "Trey". Woo, doggies! She turned into a Texas tornado, matter of fact, gave me a black eye, threatened to call Claire on the spot. I had to pull a wad of bills out to calm her down. She is one spirited filly." Bud caught himself and said, "Well, *was*, anyway."

"Had Nicki ever tried to blackmail you with this information about your affair with her?"

"Nope. Never did. I was very generous with her when we were sleepin' t'gether. I think she really appreciated the extra money, tryin' to raise that lil' kid by herself."

"What do you think would happen if Claire found out about you and Nicki?" asked Patrick.

"You 'member me talkin' 'bout a Texas tornado? That would be nuthin' compared to what Claire would do to me if she caught me cheatin' on her! After she took my hide off, she'd divorce me in a heartbeat, and leave me hangin' on the clothesline to dry!"

"Sounds like you ought to be more careful, Mr. Simpson, about other women," stated Patrick.

"Yeah," said Pete. "We wouldn't want to find you hangin' out on some old clothesline, all dried out."

Bud didn't notice the sarcasm, so Pete continued, "We don't have any other questions for you right now, but don't leave town, okay?"

"Wasn't plannin' any trips right away. You boys jest call if you wanna talk to me some more, okay? Right now I've gotta hustle out to the club to make my tee time." Bud Simpson, rose, shook their hands, and left Pete and Patrick shaking their heads at his audacity.

***

Chapter Ten

Grant McGuire was pleased with himself as he thought about the next "annoyance" he would put Tom Howell through. So far, the magazine subscriptions, the credit cards, the ipecac in the coffee, and the computer virus had simply been annoying for Tom. He was going to up the ante. Today was the practice round for the Labor Day golf tournament at Rio Grande Country Club, and he was scheduled to play in Tom's foursome. He couldn't wait!

*

Tom Howell kissed Ginger goodbye and said, "I don't know what time I'll be finished with my practice round, Babe. Looks like you're on your own for lunch."

"That's okay. I think I'll spend the morning helping Cherry input the sales figures that were lost in the computer crash. Then I need to finish typing up the lease for the office space. You do remember that we are hosting Ava Grissom for dinner tonight? We are to meet her at the club at six," replied Ginger.

"Okay. I'll probably come back to the store after golf and we can go together from there."

*

Alfred Benedetti and Ava Grissom were very busy. Even though the lease wasn't signed, activity buzzed at the office she was going to lease from the Howells. They had selected rental office furniture from Court Furniture, along with pictures, lamps, flower arrangements, rugs, and chairs for the reception area. It was to be delivered at ten o'clock this morning. The telephone company put in a priority installation at Ava's insistence, and since wiring was already in place, they had activated the phone service.

Ava had called a local business machine company. "That's right. I want the top of the line. A four in one machine that will print, scan, fax, and copy; computer with all the trimmings, including internet modem; three calculators, and oh yes, a twenty-four inch television set for the break room. No, I don't care what brand of computer. Just deliver the best. Yes! Today!" Ava turned to Al and said, "Have you called to get cable hooked up?"

"Talking to them right now," said Al, with the phone tucked under his chin.

"I wonder which one of these office supply places will deliver?" She thumbed through the yellow pages and stopped when she found an ad for Belew's Office Supply. She had made a list of necessary supplies the night before, from staplers down to the paper clips, and quickly set in motion the delivery. With each of these companies, she told them that she would like to establish an ongoing account, hinting that there would be much more to come for the Saudi Arabian Bank of Belgium.

"Did you order the coffee service, Al? I know there are places that will supply the coffee pot, and pre-packaged coffee already in the filters, and maybe we can get a vendor to place a box of candy and snacks in the break room." Ava flitted around the office space with enthusiasm, waving her hands. The long fake fingernails and cubic zirconium jewelry seemed to fascinate her, as she kept looking at her hands as she spoke.

Al watched her out of the corner of his eye as he dialed yet another vendor, and shook his head in disgust.

*

After a busy morning at the store, Ginger had just completed typing out the lease for the Saudi Arabian Bank of Belgium. "That name just floors me," she thought to herself as she picked up the folder for the lease, grabbed her purse and sweater and went down the stairs.

"I don't know how long I'll be gone, Nancy, but you can reach me on my mobile if you need me." said Ginger brightly as she went out the front door of Howell Carpets.

It was a glorious fall day. September could sometimes be wet in Albuquerque, but this week it was bright and sunny without a cloud in the sky, and there was just a hint of crispness in the air heralding the coming fall weather. *What a gorgeous day to be on the golf course...wish I were there.* Ginger headed for the parking lot. Ava had called to give her a new telephone number earlier this morning, and Ginger confirmed the appointment to sign the lease.

"Let's just meet at the office space," Ava suggested.

Ginger's face registered pure shock when she opened the door to the office that Ava was leasing.

"My Gosh! How on earth did this happen." she cried.

"Like it?" asked Ava. "We have a knack of getting things done in a hurry whenever it's necessary." she said.

"But...." began Ginger.

"I know. Isn't it wonderful?" gushed Ava. "Al and I have been on the phone since yesterday afternoon, and now I think we're ready for business, except for hiring a receptionist."

"But you haven't even signed the lease yet. And there is a little matter of first and last month's rent payment and a security deposit," said Ginger, still dubious.

"Do you have the lease with you?"

"Yes, of course," answered Ginger, pulling the lease from her briefcase. "Then I need a check for three thousand dollars for rent, plus another thousand for the deposit."

"Fine." said Ava, taking out a three ring binder of checks. "The checks have not been imprinted yet, since we were still waiting for an address, but there should be no problem." Ava took out a black pen and wrote in Saudi Arabian Bank of Belgium and the address that was on the homemade business card she was using. She then hand-wrote an account number on the bottom of the check, filled in the amount of four thousand dollars, signed the check with a flourish, and handed it to Ginger. "This might take a little while to clear, is that all right?"

Ginger looked at the check and blinked. She had never seen anything quite like this before.

Just then a deliveryman from Belew's stepped into the office with a bundle of supplies.

Thinking that this all looked very professional, Ginger responded, "Well, yes, of course. Now would you like the orientation that I give to new tenants?"

"I think I have a few minutes." She turned to her companion and said, "Al, would you please check in this delivery? I'll be back shortly." Turning to Ginger, Ava said cheerily, "Lead on McDuff."

Ginger took Ava through the building, showing her the restrooms, the telephone equipment room, and lastly, how to operate the alarm system on the entry doors. "If you spend any time here on the weekend, you will need to know how to disarm and to re-set the alarm system," said Ginger. "With the murder that took place at the club Monday night, I think it underscores the need for security."

"Yes, I heard about that waitress. She was so young, too."

Ginger nodded. "There is a button here that allows you to lock yourself in the building. Anyone that enters without the code will set off the alarm." She walked Ava through the process of setting the alarm, disarming it, and bypassing it if she wanted to lock herself inside.

"I think I've got it." said Ava, waving her hands around and watching them as she spoke. "Thank you so much for your patience, Ginger, and I'll be looking forward to dinner tonight. Six o'clock, right?"

"Yes. Tom and I are looking forward to it."

"I think the business machines are being delivered, so I've got to get back upstairs. See you later."

Ginger was still rather stunned by this whirling dervish, and stood for a moment watching her ascend the stairs. She looked at the check that was still in her hand. *I wonder what my banker is going to say about this?*

Ginger did not see Alfred Benedetti as he stood silently gazing at her from the balcony on the second floor. He didn't move or say anything as he frowned at her, and followed her with his steely eyes until she exited the building.

*

Pamela Johnson always slept late. Since her husband had died and her affinity for Scotch had been born, she had a bit of trouble getting up and around in the mornings. This particular morning was different. She raised Yorkshire terrier show dogs and there was a dog show this afternoon. She had to get her precious dogs groomed and ready for the show.

Pamela still mourned the little bitch that she had to put down the week before. Mrs. Johnson's Penelope Queen had been her very favorite and an AKC Champion, but old age had taken her sight and her hearing, and she suffered from arthritis and frequent kidney stones. Pamela had no choice but to give her the shot of sodium pentobarbital that was the most humane animal euthanasia.

Her eyes filled with tears as she thought of her tiny little Penelope Queen and what a great show dog she had been. She reached for a tissue to wipe her eyes and blow her nose, then she fortified herself with "just a little nip" of Scotch, and went to get the first tiny dog for her bath and grooming.

"C'mon, little Sweetums," she said, taking the first little dog out of her cage. "You'll need to really look sharp today to catch the judge's eye."

*

Tom Howell, Grant McGuire, Bud Simpson, and Antonio Ciccone were paired for the practice round for the golf tournament at Rio Grande Country Club. Bud had not met Grant or Dr. Ciccone before, so when they met on the first tee box, they shook hands and introduced themselves.

"Bud Simpson, originally from Texas, as if you couldn't tell." said Bud in his native Texas drawl. "I know Tom, of course, but don't think I've had the pleasure of meeting you other two."

"Grant McGuire. I was a college roommate of Tom's," stated Grant. "And I've been trying to keep up with him ever since." There was more truth than fiction in Grant's comment, even though he said it offhandedly.

"Dr. Antonio Ciccone. On the golf course, I go by "Tony". Pleased to meet you both. Tom and I have known each other for quite a while and I'm sure that I have seen both of you around the club at different times."

"Tony Ciccone! That has a nice ring to it," smiled Bud. Dr. Ciccone grimaced. He had always hated it when the kids on the playground had teased him with the name.

"Well, with those introductions out of the way, let's tee off," and with that comment, Tom teed up his ball.

Bud Simpson glanced at Grant, remembered what he had told the homicide detective, and made a mental note to call Pete Lucero as soon as they finished the eighteen holes. He thought he remembered seeing Nicki at the club with a tall man who had salt and pepper hair. Grant McGuire was that man. He and Claire had danced the night away, Nicki had finished her shift, and Grant McGuire came in and sat down with her at one of the back tables. Both of them looked as if they were in la-la land. *Information like this should keep suspicion off me. Maybe Homicide Detective Lucero can connect Grant to Nicki's drug habit.*

*

"Holy cow!" Ginger Howell was shocked for the second time today. She picked up the mail from the front desk at the store and found a small envelope addressed to Tom. Nicolette du Pree's name was written as the return address on the envelope. Realizing that Tom was on the golf course, and wouldn't want to be distracted, Ginger weighed the consequences of calling him on his cell phone. He would probably have put it on "vibrate" rather than "ring" so it wouldn't disturb anyone else. She decided that this was important enough that Tom would want to be informed, even if he was on the golf course. Knowing how he jumped every time it buzzed on his hip, she went ahead and dialed the number, hoping that he wasn't in his backswing.

When the phone vibrated on his belt loop, Tom jumped as if he had been shot, as usual. The four men had just teed off and were heading to their carts when it buzzed him. Tom held back until Grant was in the cart before he answered.

"Yo," he said as he opened the flip-phone.

"Tom, it's Ginger. I just got the mail from the front desk. There is an envelope here addressed to you—and it's from Nicki! I thought you should know about it."

"Well," said Tom quietly. "Open it up and see what she had to say." said Tom, as the surprise registered on his face.

"Okay," said Ginger, as she quickly sliced the top of the envelope with a letter opener. "It's very short. She says, "Mr. Howell, I know that you will do what is right. If something happens to me, talk to Bertha." and it is signed Nicolette du Pree."

"I have no idea who "Bertha" is, Ginger. Why don't you come on out to the club early and talk to Paula, the waitress that worked with Nicki. See if she knows anything about a "Bertha". We need to check it out before calling Lucero. I've gotta run, we're due to hit our second shots now. I'll see you in a few hours. Love you, bye." Tom didn't wait for Ginger to respond before he hung up.

Grant heard only "Lucero" and instantly pricked up his ears. "Problem, Tom?" he asked.

"Nothing that Ginger can't handle," replied Tom. "Now, where did you hit your drive?" he asked as he drove down the cart path. Grant frowned at Tom's answer, but simply pointed at the right rough, the direction he had sliced his drive.

*

Ginger didn't waste any time getting out to the club, hoping that Paula would just be coming to work for the noon shift in the lounge. Luck seemed to be on her side. Paula was the first person Ginger saw when she walked into the lounge.

"Good morning, Mrs. Howell. Would you like a menu?" asked Paula.

"No, thank you, Paula. As a matter of fact, I really just need to talk to you for a moment. It's about Nicki."

"Oh," Paula's face showed despair. "I've told the detectives everything I know about that night—and about Nicki."

"Paula, Tom got a letter from Nicki in the mail today. Please don't mention it to anyone, but I need to ask if you know a woman named Bertha?"

"Oh. She must have mailed it before that night!"

"I'm sure she did. Can you help me with information about Bertha?"

Paula breathed a sigh of relief. "Oh, yes, of course. Bertha is Nicki's nanny. She came here with Nicki from Florida, and takes care of Nicki's little boy, Trey. Nicki talked to me about her all the time. I guess she is a pretty special woman, at least in Nicki's eyes."

"That's good news. I'm sure that it will be important for Trey to have someone around that he knows and trusts. Do you know how I can get in touch with her?"

"I suppose she is still at the house. Nicki leased a place not too far from the club so she could run home and see Trey on her break.

"Do you remember the address of the house?"

"Nicki took me with her one day to meet Trey. He is such a darling child—looks exactly like his mother. I'm sure I remember the address."

Paula wrote the address down on a napkin and handed it to Ginger.

"Thanks, Paula. Maybe Bertha has some information that she didn't tell the police. It might be useful in finding out who killed Nicki."

"Did Nicki's letter say why you needed to contact Bertha?"

"No, it didn't," replied Ginger, "but thank you very much for the information. Maybe it will help in some way."

"I'm still in shock over what happened. It's a little scary, although I don't really think the rest of us are in danger."

"By the way, Paula, did Nicki say anything to you about overhearing a conversation that she wasn't supposed to hear?"

"No. Sorry."

***

In Total Darkness

Chapter Eleven

Tom Howell, Grant McGuire, Bud Simpson, and Antonio Ciccone finished their golf round, posted their scores, and went into the lounge for drinks.

"Hi Paula, I guess the drinks are on me, since I won the bets," said Tom. "I'll have a cola. Bring these gentlemen whatever they would like."

"I'll have a lite beer—one of those Rocky Mountain types—in a can," said Grant.

"Same for me," echoed Bud.

"A glass of white wine, please," resounded Tony's deep voice, as he smiled at Paula.

"Thank you, gentlemen, I'll have these for you right away," said Paula, pleasantly.

"Nice looking girl," said Tony, watching her walk away.

"Might as well back off, Tony," murmured Grant. "I've already tried—no dice. I think she is married. *Really* married." Tony frowned at him.

"If you'll excuse me, I need to make a phone call," said Bud. "Gotta check in with th' little woman. Be right back."

Bud left the lounge to use the telephone in the lobby. He wanted to call Pete Lucero now that he knew Grant McGuire was the man he had seen with Nicki.

The receptionist with the angel's voice answered Bud's call.

"Homicide Division, may I ask who is calling?"
"This is Bud Simpson. Detective Pete Lucero, please."
"I'm very sorry, Mr. Simpson, but Detective Lucero is out of the office at this time. I can take a message, or give you his voice mail."
"Just tell him that I called, and I have the name of the man that I saw with Nicolette du Pree."
"Yes, sir. Anything else?"
"Just have him call me."
Bud returned to the table quickly after leaving the message for Pete to call him.

Five minutes later, Ginger walked into the lounge and made a beeline for Tom's table. "There you are, Tom. Hello, fellows, do you mind very much if I borrow my husband? If you are all finished here, I have made an appointment for us, and we need to leave right away," said Ginger.

"Why don't you take him and never let him come back again." spouted Grant. "He beat me again--by four strokes."

"Your honey is a purty danged good golfer, Miz Howell," said Bud.

"Good to see you again, Ginger. Tom has had no lasting effects from the ipecac, as I presumed. At least it didn't hurt his golf game today." said Tony.

"Sounds like you had a pretty good score, Tom, judging from these comments. Hope you weren't too rough on them," Ginger smiled at her husband. "And now, guys, we've got to leave or we'll never make it on time. Tom, my car is parked just outside. Let's go in it."

Grant McGuire watched as the couple walked out of the lounge and was already deciding what dirty trick he would pull on Tom next.

"What's the rush, Gin?" asked Tom, as soon as they were out of earshot. "Were you able to find out anything about "Bertha"?"

"Yes, and that's why we are in a hurry. When I asked Paula, she said that Bertha was Nicki's nanny. She came here from Florida with Nicki to be a nanny for Trey. When I called her to set this appointment, she sounded scared. If Nicki told her about the conversation she overheard, she might also be in danger. I think we need to hurry."

It didn't take them long to make the short trip from the club to Nicki's house. A gray-haired lady wearing an apron over her dress opened the door when they rang the bell. She looked worried, the tension showing through the wrinkles in her skin.

"I'm Ginger Howell. You must be Bertha," said Ginger. "I called you earlier."

"Please come in, Mrs. Howell. I guess this is your husband?"

"Yes, this is Tom. Nicki called him a few hours before she was killed."

Bertha quickly looked around outside as if to check and see if anyone had followed the Howells. She asked them to come in and then immediately closed the door and started crying.

"Poor Miss Nicki," sobbed the old lady. "It shouldn't have ever happened!"

"Please, Bertha, we want to help anyway we can to find out who did this to Nicki. She must have thought that you could help us, if anything bad happened to her." Ginger pulled out the letter that Nicki had written to Tom. "What can you tell us, Bertha?" said Ginger as she handed the letter to the old lady.

"Please sit down," said Bertha as she read the note. "Nicki told me about overhearing two men, talking about providing drugs for some very influential politicians in Albuquerque and Santa Fe."

"Did she mention any names, Bertha?" asked Tom.

"Maybe I'd recognize a name if I heard it." She paused as if trying to remember. "I wasn't paying a lot of attention, but she did say that one of the men had been providing her with cocaine, and the other one was prominent in the New Mexico

State Legislature. She knew that I disapproved of the drug use, and she promised me that she would quit. Only one more time, she said. Just one more time. I'm afraid that I was more interested in what she was saying about quitting the drugs than what she had overheard." Bertha broke into tears again.

"Drugs and politics can be a deadly combination, Bertha. If anyone knows that Nicki may have talked to you there is a possibility that you could also be in danger. Is there any place that you can go until this whole thing is solved?"

"We have no one here in Albuquerque. It was just Nicki, Trey, and I, trying to make a new life out here after we left Florida," said Bertha worriedly.

"Bertha, would you be willing to bring Trey down to my house and stay with us for a while? I am concerned for your safety, and I am sure that you would never go anywhere without the little boy," said Tom gently.

"You mean stay at your house?"

"Exactly. Our housekeeper, Maggie, would be delighted to have the company and she loves children, especially little boys."

"Well....I don't know..."

"If it occurs to the killer that Nicki may have talked to you, then you are in danger. Who would be left to take care of Trey if something happened to you?"

Bertha looked into Tom's eyes and could see that he was a man to be trusted. And besides, Miss Nicki said he would do the right thing.

"When would you want us to go?" she asked.

"Right now. Before anyone comes looking for you."

"Tom that is a great idea! Why don't you gather up enough clothes for you and the little boy for about a week, Bertha? I might sneak back over here for anything you forget."

She stood up and said, "I'll help you. Do you have a suitcase handy? If not, just some grocery sacks will work for part of the clothing, and we can hang the rest in the back of my car."

Ginger noticed that Trey had come into the room. He was about three to four years old, and had his mother's big green eyes, flaming red hair, and just a sprinkling of freckles across his nose. He didn't say anything, but just looked at Tom and Ginger as if to determine if they were good guys or bad guys. When they smiled at him, he decided they must be good guys.

"You must be Trey." smiled Ginger. "What a fine looking young man you are. Would you like to visit with us for a few days at our house in the valley?"

"Will my mother be there?" he asked.

Ginger's heart wrenched. She looked up at Tom, then at Bertha. Bertha shook her head. It was apparent that she had not told Trey that his mother would not be coming back.

"She is not there, Trey, but I think that she would want you to come with us," said Ginger very gently, as she kneeled down to meet the little boy on his level. "We have some wonderful peacocks that would be fun for you to see. How about it?"

"Bertha can come, too?" he asked.

"Of course Bertha will come," offered Tom.

Trey smiled for the first time. "That sounds like fun!"

Ginger took Trey by the hand and said, "Why don't you show me your bedroom, and we'll pick out some fun clothes for you to wear."

Tom motioned for Bertha to wait a moment, then quietly said, "I think that it would be a good idea for me to call the homicide detectives. They may want to look through the house to see if there are any clues as to the identity of the person selling drugs to Nicki. If you don't mind, I'll give them a call."

Bertha nodded, and then quickly left to join Ginger and Trey in the bedroom.

Tom pulled up Pete Lucero's telephone number from his cell phone, having entered it in the address book after Ginger dialed him earlier in the week.

"Homicide, this is Lucero," he answered on the first ring.

"Pete, it's Tom Howell. Something has come up that you need to know about."

"Shoot."

"I got a letter from Nicolette du Pree in the mail today."

"No kidding! Anything in it that could be useful?"

"No names. However, she did mention that we should talk to her nanny. Ginger and I are at her house now, and plan to take Bertha and Nicki's little boy down to the estate to stay with us until all of this blows over."

"Why would you do that?"

"Nicki apparently overheard a conversation that got her killed. If the killer thinks she might have told the nanny about the conversation, then I think she and the little boy might also be in danger."

"When is this going to take place?"

"As soon as we can get a few clothes together and get them out of here. I thought that you might want to process this house just in case Nicki left some clue as to where she was getting her drugs."

"We had planned to check out her house right away."

"We will leave the key to the house under a rock by the front porch."

"What is that address? I'm sure that Patrick has it from the employee files, but it would be good to have it handy." Tom told him the address.

"There's a possibility that we could be there within the hour. Thanks for filling us in on the information. We will need to see the letter, of course."

"I'll make it a point to bring it by sometime in the morning," responded Tom.

"Did the nanny tell you what Nicki overheard? Names?"

"There were some names, but Bertha was more interested in what Nicki had to say about quitting the drugs than in the names of people she didn't know. At this time she just can't remember."

"Sometimes these names will pop up when you are not really thinking about them. You might mention that to the lady."

"Good thinking. By the way, Pete, do you have a time of death, or cause of death, yet?"

"Time of death was about 9:15. The other waitress said that Nicki took her break at nine o'clock and never did come back. She remembered exactly when Nicki was supposed to be back to work, and it really hacked her off when she didn't show up for the rest of her shift. We don't want it out on the street, yet, but yes, we do have the cause of death. She was put to sleep."

"*What?*"

"Literally. Someone injected her with sodium pentobarbital, the solution that they use to put animals to sleep."

Tom was so astounded that he didn't immediately reply.

"Anyway, thanks for the information. I know from experience that you and Ginger can be a big help. If you hear anything else that might be relevant, don't hesitate to call me."

"You got it," said Tom. He waited to share this information with Ginger until after Bertha and Trey were safely delivered to the Howell estate.

***

In Total Darkness

Chapter Twelve

It didn't take long to get Bertha and Trey settled into a guest suite at the Howell estate. Maggie was delighted to have company, and the three of them were deep into a discussion about what kind of cookies they would bake when Tom and Ginger left for the club.

"We won't be home for dinner tonight, Maggie, so you three just take your time and get acquainted," said Ginger.

Bertha followed them to the door. She looked very serious when she quietly replied, "Thank you so much. I was so worried about Trey. This will help take his mind off his mama. I know I'm going to have to tell him she won't be coming back. I've just been avoiding it. Maybe now...."

"I am sure you will find the right time to tell him, Bertha," replied Ginger. "The Lord helps us get through these tough times, if we'll just ask Him."

Ginger's eyes were misty as she took Tom's arm, and the pair left for the club.

*

Ava Grissom was still dressed in the velvet sweat pants and top she had been wearing that morning. She greeted Tom and Ginger at the front door of the club, enthusiastically waving her hands around.

"There you are. I do want to apologize for my attire. There wasn't any time to go home and change clothes with all the deliveries we had today."

"You look fine," said Tom. "I'd still be in golf clothes if Gin hadn't insisted I shower and change."

"You *have* been busy today, haven't you," stated Ginger. The trio headed back toward the dining room, exchanging pleasantries and discussing the fantastic weather that had settled into the valley.

"Good evening, Paula," said Ginger to the waitress. "My goodness, you must work all the time. Don't they ever give you any time off?"

Paula smiled and replied, "When you have a couple of kids all the time they can give me helps with the bills. Are you ready to order?"

The trio placed their orders and sipped on their drinks until the food was delivered. They didn't bring up the business of the office building until after they had eaten and the dishes had been cleared away.

"Now, Ms. Grissom, I would really like to hear about this bank you are working for, and the type of business you are running," said Tom.

"You must call me Ava," she said, as she pulled out a cigarette holder and inserted a cigarette into the end of it. "Do you mind if I smoke?"

Tom raised one eyebrow and stole a glance at Ginger, who was frowning slightly. Then he said, "I don't mind a bit, but I don't think they allow smoking in the dining room any longer. They might throw us out on our ears."

Ava silently put away the cigarette holder. "That's all right. I need to cut down anyway. Now, about the bank—I'm certain that it is rather confusing for Americans to understand. I started working for the Sheik about six years ago while I was on an educational junket in Saudi Arabia. I loved the people and the work. They promoted me right up through the ranks, even though it's unusual for them to pay much attention to a woman.

"I've read that women's lib is pretty non-existent in the Middle East," said Ginger.

Ava nodded. "About two months ago, the Sheik decided he would like to set up a field of operations here in the States. You can imagine my delight when he selected me to be in charge of the operation. He gave me carte blanche to set up an office and begin operations."

"Very interesting," murmured Tom. "And now that you have an office, what kind of business will the bank be operating?"

"Loans, Tom, loans. We operate on the profits from arbitrage dealings. We don't make any loans for less than one million dollars, American," stated Ava firmly.

"Arbitrage, huh?" Tom rubbed his chin. "If I remember my college economics class, an arbitrage would be the simultaneous purchase of the same securities, commodities, or moneys in different markets, hoping to profit from unequal prices. Is that about right?"

"You have a good memory, Tom. That is exactly how it works. The kicker is the loan business. There is a finder's fee for a loan of this magnitude, and the Sheik decides which applicants he will accept. He may loan up to five or six million dollars to an applicant, if he feels they are a worthy client."

"What kind of finder's fee are you thinking?"

Ava tapped her long fake fingernails on the table. It seemed she might be getting a bit nervous under Tom's questioning. "The fee is due in advance and has been between $25,000.00 and $200,000.00 in the cases where I have been involved."

"What happens to the fee if the loan is not approved?" asked Ginger.

"Unfortunately, it is forfeited. There is quite a lot of red tape in securing the loan, you see."

"Wow! That's a lot of fee to be forfeited," exclaimed Ginger. "Especially for someone that needs a loan in the first place."

The discussion continued, with several references to the experiences Ava had while living in Saudi Arabia, as well as the names of the bigger clients that the Saudi Arabian Bank of Belgium served. "Of course, you have never heard of them but they are really well-known in the Middle-East."

Tom and Ginger gradually began to excuse themselves from the conversation, thanked Ava for the lease, and rose to leave. "I'm sorry to cut this short, Ava, but if I intend to give my competitors a run for their money in this golf tournament tomorrow I've got to get some rest tonight," stated Tom. As they left, Ava was ordering another glass of Cabernet Sauvignon…on Tom's tab, of course.

*

"Well, Hon, what's your take on Ms. Ava?" asked Ginger.

"I might be wrong, Gin, but that sounds like the biggest crock of garbage I've ever heard." He paused. "If you had not gotten a check from her for the lease, I'd suggest you send her packing," said Tom, earnestly.

"Tom, you ought to see what she has done with the office," cried Ginger. "She had it totally furnished, clear up to the pictures on the wall before I got there this morning with the lease to sign. It looks as if they have been there for weeks." She reached into her purse for the check Ava had given her. "This *did* look a bit weird to me, though," she said as she handed the check to Tom.

"Good grief." Tom was shocked as he looked at the handwritten numbers on the check. "Well, one thing for sure, if the check doesn't clear, we'll sure have her on a bogus check charge."

"It certainly will be interesting to see what the bank has to say about it," stated Ginger, rather glumly. "Oh, I almost forgot. Since you left your car here when we went to see Bertha, we'll have to go home in separate cars."

"Well, we'll meet you at the pass, then, amigo," said Tom, in his best John Wayne imitation. However, he wasn't prepared for what he found when he got to his car in the parking lot out by the pro shop. He noticed immediately that the both tires on the driver's side of the car were flat.

"Oh, damn! What the hell is going on around here?" When he walked around to the other side of the car, his shoulders drooped as he found the other two tires were flat as well. A sinking feeling hit the pit of his stomach. It was really beginning to bug him, all of this nonsense—for no particular reason. He had no idea who would want to harass him this badly. With a deep sigh, he pulled out his cell phone and called Ginger's mobile telephone number.

"Would you mind coming back to the club to get me, Ginger?" said Tom irritably.

"What's wrong?" asked Ginger. "Car won't start?"

"Just come get me!" he yelled as he snapped his flip-phone shut.

Ginger had not gotten very far toward home when she got Tom's call, so it only took her five minutes to be back in the parking lot.

"Oh," she said, as Tom got into the passenger side of her car. "Flat tire?"

"Make it *four* flat tires, Babe. *Four!* This is another intentional slap at me, *personally*! I just wish that whoever is upset with me would talk to me in person about whatever is bothering them. Of all the low down…"

Ginger interrupted him. "I can't believe it. It *is* getting ridiculous. We're just going to have to figure out the name of this pervert." She stole a glance over at her husband, his handsome face contorted into a frown, eyes blazing with anger. "Maybe it's someone that doesn't want you to beat him in the tournament tomorrow, and is just trying to distract you," she offered. Tom didn't reply.

"Can you remember the number for the service station we use?" he asked.

"Sure." Ginger told him the number.

Tom dialed the number and arranged for a service truck to come out and fix all four flat tires. He would leave the car in the parking lot, so he would have it available after the second round of the tournament. Ginger could drop him off in the morning.

*

The Lexus pulled up behind a group of cottonwood trees on a dirt road down in the bosque. The man switched off the lights and settled his rotund frame down in the comfortable seat to wait. He impatiently pulled at the corner of his dark mustache. Drumming his fingers on the edge of the steering wheel, he squinted his beady eyes at the road and watched for another car. He didn't have long to wait.

The old car that pulled up beside him was covered with mud, its license plate unreadable. The man in the old car got out, walked up to the Lexus, and tapped on the window.

The window was noiseless as it slid down into the door. "Have you got the stuff?" asked the man in the Lexus.

"Sure thing, Senator. I wouldn't let ya down. You know you can count on me," said the other man.

"You took care of that red-headed bitch who heard us talking?"

"She sure was a pretty little thing. Too bad she had big ears. Quite a waste, don't you think?"

"She talks to the cops, or the press, and you wouldn't think it was a waste. We'd all be dead meat," replied the Senator vehemently. "You think she had a chance to talk to anyone?"

"I don't think so, but I overheard someone talking about a nanny. I might need to check that out."

"You should have already taken care of that! We've got some big names under the gun here—going clear up into the

Roundhouse in Santa Fe—some District Court judges here in town, too," shouted the pudgy man in the Lexus.

"I plan to go by the red-head's house as soon as I leave here. By the way, it may be a few days before I can connect with you again. I have to make a quick trip to Juarez, and I need to do it without blowing my cover."

"*Your* cover! Do you realize what they'll do to *me* if the narcs get hold of this connection? And I'll tell you, I won't go down by myself," said the senator nervously. "You just make sure you don't get caught!"

"Cool your jets, man! Things are working out pretty smoothly right now, and we don't have any reason to think that anyone can put any of us together. I'll send a signal as soon as I get back from Mexico."

The man in the Lexus handed a fat envelope full of cash to the other one, who in return handed the senator a large manila envelope filled with small plastic bags full of illegal drugs. Once the exchange was made, they pulled away in opposite directions, waiting for several hundred yards before turning on their headlights.

When the man left the Senator in the bosque, he immediately headed for Nicki's house. He was worried now about this nanny of hers. Women tend to talk too much. If she told her nanny what she overheard, that old lady would be dangerous to the "operation". He had to find her before she could repeat that information to anyone.

The windows were dark when he pulled up in front of the house. He closed the car door without a sound and quietly walked around the perimeter of the house. Not a sound. No lights. No visible vehicle, but one might be in the garage.

He walked up to the front door and rang the bell. No answer. He jammed his hands into his pockets. He might check with the neighbors to see if they had talked to the old woman and knew where she was. *"I have to find out where the old lady has gone. The Senator won't put up with mistakes, and neither will the Boss,"* he thought silently. It seemed that waiting too long to check out this possibility of being "fingered" was a bad mistake.

*

Grant McGuire smiled to himself as he opened yet another beer, propped up his feet on the coffee table, and flipped on the TV with the remote control. He relished the fact that Tom Howell would find his precious car with four flat tires. He had made sure that no one had seen him as he pulled his vehicle over by Tom's car, and swiftly poked his knife into each tire in turn. They made a spewing sound but the parking lot was empty and he felt sure he had not been seen. Maybe that would be enough distraction to keep Tom off his golf game tomorrow, he thought as he zapped the commercial that had come on.

He briefly considered calling a lady friend to see if she might come over and keep him company, but decided that he might need to just hang out and relax tonight. "I'm going to give ol' Tom a run for his money on the golf course tomorrow," he chuckled then pulled his feet off the table, slipped off his boots, flipped to another channel on the television, and frowned as he realized that he had already drained this last can of beer. Maybe he'd have just *one* more.

*

Bud Simpson wanted to divert any attention away from himself when it came to any connection with Nicki. Claire was beginning to ask questions. He didn't want Claire to ask questions. She had always believed everything he told her, but lately she had given him a funny look and was asking him to explain things. If Claire ever found out he'd had an affair with Nicki, or any of those other girls, she'd divorce him so quick it'd make his head swim. He always told everyone that it was his Daddy who owned the oil wells in Texas, but it was really Claire who had inherited all the money...money he had spent liberally. He had run through quite a few million bucks she'd inherited from dear old Daddy, but there was still enough left that she'd never miss what he had spent. He just couldn't have her asking questions, and he certainly couldn't have her snooping into his laptop computer. That little spitfire, Nicki, just might have wanted to spill the beans if he hadn't shelled out the bucks to keep her quiet. He had to make sure Nicki had not left anything in the motor home, and since she was dead then he should be in the clear.

He ought to be hearing from that detective Lucero any minute now.

When the phone rang, Bud let it ring three times before he answered it, to make sure that his voice was strong and clear.

"Mr. Simpson, this is Homicide Detective Pete Lucero. I have a message that you called me," said Pete.

"That's right. Can I call you Pete?"

"Sure."

"Well, Pete, it's about that cute lil' red-headed waitress, Nicolette du Pree. Do you remember asking me 'bout where I thought she might be gettin' her drugs?"

"Of course. You have a name for me?"

"Well, this guy may not be *sellin'* them to her, but they sure could be *usin'* them together. When I saw them they both looked "stoned". Anyway, damned if I didn't get paired with the guy for today's golf round. His name is Grant McGuire." stated Bud firmly.

"Grant McGuire? Other than looking "stoned" tell me why you think he might have a drug connection to Nicki."

"Well, Claire and I just *love* to dance. We were down at the club a week or so ago, dancin' up a storm. They had this lil' combo that was playin' western music, you know, Two-Step, Cotton-Eyed-Joe, line dancin'—that sort of thing, you know?"

"I'm not familiar with the dances, but go ahead with the story."

"Well, we were about the only couple left dancin'; all the waitresses had gone off shift; and I noticed lil' Nicki sittin' all by herself at one of th' back tables, when all of a sudden this Grant-fella comes in, looks around like he was huntin' someone, spots Nicki, and wobbles right over to her table. There was too much music noise for me to hear whut they said to each other from that distance, but Nicki had this kinda "dreamy" look on her face, kinda like she was high on somethin', and this Grant-fella looked like he was feelin' no pain, ya know whut I mean?"

"You think he was drunk?" asked Pete.

"Well, I don't know th' recipe, but the cake mighta been baked in th' same oven, if ya know whut I mean."

"Under the influence of something?"

"I'd bet my bottom dollar on it!" stated Bud.

"Did you go over and speak to them?"

"Hell, no! Not with Claire by my side. I don't want Claire to think that I even notice lil' chicks like Nicki," stated Bud vehemently.

There was silence on the phone as Pete thought about what Bud had told him.

"Is there anything else you'd like to tell me?" asked Pete.

"Nope. That's it. Said I'd call, so I called," said Bud.

"Thank you for the information Mr. Simpson. It looks like we might have to talk to Mr. McGuire," said Pete.

***

Chapter Thirteen

The autumn sun shined brightly through Pete Lucero's office window, mocking the dark mood that had settled into his mind. His stomach growled, reminding him that he hadn't eaten breakfast...again. His stomach was not only empty, but also burning; a precursor to the ulcer that he knew he deserved. "Carmen, I don't know how you could do this to me," he muttered under his breath, wishing she had not taken the kids and left him. She just didn't understand this cop business, he thought. It just doesn't run on a scheduled eight to five day. Not only was his mood dark, but also the junipers had touched off his seasonal allergies, making him miserable. He groaned as he looked at the pile of folders on his desk, took another swig of the battery acid in his cup that was pretending to be coffee, and hit the intercom button.

"Patrick? Have you got a minute?" he asked into the speaker.

"Sure, Pete. Let me finish printing this one last file. I'll be right there," he answered.

Patrick Mahoney could be the poster boy for the Ultimate Irish Policeman. When he smiled, his blue eyes sparkled with vivacity, making him utterly adorable to the ladies. Married for less than a year, he fit the husband role comfortably. He hit "Print", waited on the report to chug its way into a pile, picked up the papers and headed into Pete's office.

"Good grief, Pete, you look like a truck ran over you on the way to work this morning." exclaimed Patrick.

"That's exactly the way I feel, too," responded Pete.

"These damned allergies. I'd like to dig out every juniper in town and burn them. However, I don't think that our case is going to wait for me to sneeze and wheeze my way through this season...so, what have you got on the list of those people who have access to sodium pentobarbital?"

"Amazing what Dora can do." He used his pet nickname for his computer. "I contacted the pharmaceutical supply companies and got a customer list—at least the ones that had any orders for sodium pentobarbital. Except for a few medical doctors, most of them are veterinarians. Then I entered the member list from Rio Grande Country Club, and all of their employees, too. I had the computer to cross-match and come up with any names that were on both lists. There were only three. One of them, Arnold Johnson, passed away about a year ago. The membership at the country club is still in his name, so maybe the wife still belongs and just hasn't taken her husband off the list. Then I called the office for the other one and hit a dead end there. He left three weeks ago for a European cruise and won't be back until the end of October. Oh yes, Dr. Antonio Ciccone's name was on both lists as well."

"Why don't we call the dead man's wife and see about the status of the business. You have her name and number on that report?" asked Pete.

Patrick ran his finger quickly down one of the lists. "Here it is. Widow's name is Pamela, and here's the number."

Pete dialed quickly, and while the phone was ringing, he took the opportunity to blow his nose again.

"Hel...loo.oo," hiccupped Pamela Johnson, answering the phone. It was apparent that she had already been drinking. Pete looked at his watch. Nine twenty-five in the morning.

"Mrs. Johnson? Pete Lucero. I am a Homicide Detective with APD. I'd like to ask you a few questions."

"Quesss…shuns? What for?" slurred Pamela.

"Maybe we should come out to see you in person, Mrs. Johnson," responded Pete, rolling his eyes at Patrick.

"Tha'ss all righ'. You can ashk me now," said Pamela.

"Well, the first question is about your husband's business. We understand that he passed away about a year ago?" queried Pete.

"Yesss," slurred Pamela.

"We are interested in what happened to the business after your husband passed away. Did you sell it to another vet or just close it down?"

Pamela cleared her throat. "You sheee, (hic) my husband's offish is out in the back of our houshh. No way would I everrr let an(hic)other vet work out there."

"And what happened to the pharmaceuticals that he had in his possession when he died?"

"They're schtill there. Righ' where my poor (hic) Arnold left them." At the mention of Arnold's name, Pamela's voice choked up and tears welled up in her eyes.

"Mrs. Johnson, I think my partner and I need to come take a look at your husband's office. Would it be all right if we came over now?"

"Of coursh," she replied. "It will be nicsh to have guests over. I'll make shome fresh coffee." She was making an effort to sound sober.

It didn't take Pete Lucero and Patrick Mahoney but fifteen minutes to reach the Johnson home. "I hope that she remembers that we are coming," said Pete fervently. "She was three sheets in the wind already."

Patrick frowned, "Three sheets, partner? What's that all about?"

"Never mind," said Pete, pushing the doorbell.

They heard a voice calling, "Coming. I'm coming." They weren't ready for what they saw when the door opened.

Pamela Johnson had slipped on a long silk robe with ostrich feather trim down the lapels on both sides. The shoe on her left foot didn't match the one on the right. She had twisted up her long gray-blond hair into a messy knot that was held in place by a pencil sticking through it. Her attempt at putting on her make-up had failed miserably, with smeared mascara, rouge on one cheek and not the other, and she had almost missed her mouth with the lipstick.

"Mrs. Johnson?" said Pete with a question in his voice.

"Oh, do come in." Pamela grabbed Pete by the elbow and pulled him into the entryway. "The coffee is almoss ready. She stumbled slightly and held onto Pete's arm a bit more firmly. "Come right thesh way."

Patrick had no choice but to follow the two into the kitchen.

"Mrs. Johnson, we really just need to see your husband's office," said Patrick politely.

"Fine. Righ' after you've had your (hic) coffee." Pamela rattled three china cups and saucers, a sugar bowl, and a creamer from the hutch. She managed to partially fill the creamer with milk from the refrigerator, spilling only a few drops, then got spoons to set by each cup. As she started to pick up the coffee pot, Patrick stepped up politely and said, "Would you allow me to pour, Mrs. Johnson?" He then took the pot, filled the three cups, and returned the coffee pot to the counter.

"What a nisch young man," said Pamela, blinking.

As they drank their coffee, Pete took the opportunity to ask another question.

"Mrs. Johnson, do you know anything about a drug called sodium pentobarbital?"

"Oh, of courshe," she slurred. "Tha's wha' you usch t' put aminals down. I've seen my hushban' do it many times. They jus' go righ' to schleep while he's talkin' to them ver' gently. They never see it comin'." She started to cry. "Tha's wha' I did for my poor lil' Penelope Queen!"

"Who is Penelope Queen?" asked Patrick.

"She was my lil' AKC Champion Yorkie. I had to put her to sleep las' week!" Pamela started sobbing.

"You know how to use the drug for that?" asked Pete.

"Oh, yesss."

Setting his coffee cup back into its saucer, Pete said, "I think we need to see that office, now."

They were a bit surprised at the tidiness of the office. Everything was completely spotless and organized. The drug cabinet, which contained numerous vials of medications, was closed, but unlocked. There were several bottles of sodium pentobarbital, and syringes for injecting it.

"I think that we will have to take one of these bottles with us, Mrs. Johnson, as possible evidence."

"Evidence of wha'?" she asked.

"It's possible that one of these bottles and a needle like this was used to kill Nicki du Pree. Did you know Ms. du Pree?"

Weaving slightly as she walked to the chair at the back of the desk, she replied, "You mean tha' lil' red-headed trollop masqueradin' as a waitress at the club?" Pete raised one eyebrow and nodded. "Yep, I knew who she wasss…and she knew *all* of the men!" Pamela winked at Patrick.

On the way back to their office, Pete turned to Patrick and said, "We need to make a note to have somebody from the State go over and secure those drugs."

"No kidding!" averred Patrick.

***

Chapter Fourteen

Michael Stevens looked at the card on his desk and dialed Jon Howell.

"Howell Homes, this is Jon," was the response.

"Hello, Jon. Michael Stevens. I am the assistant manager at Rio Grande Country Club. We met the other night. I wanted to set an appointment with you to look at a set of plans for an addition to the building here."

"Sounds interesting. I am available this afternoon. Would three-thirty be a good time for you?"

"Perfect. I'll see you at three-thirty."

Judith's desk was just across the room from Jon's. She couldn't help but overhear the conversation, shook her head slightly and said gently, "You do remember that you are supposed to pick up Sydney from cheerleader practice, don't you?" she asked.

"Not a problem. I'll pick her up at three twenty-five and take her with me to meet Stevens. She can surely find something to do for the few minutes that I spend with him."

*

While Jon met with Michael Stevens, Sydney wandered down to the golf pro shop to look at the women's golf clothes.

Just then she spotted her grandfather, Tom Howell coming out of the men's locker room. She hurried out to meet him.

"Hi, Popsy!" she ran up to Tom, leaned up on tiptoe to put her arms around his neck to give him a big hug.

"Syd! What a nice surprise! What are you doing here?" exclaimed Tom, returning her hug.

"Dad is meeting with Mr. Stevens about some construction or something. Are you finished with your round?"

"Just making the turn, Sweetheart. I'm in the middle of a tournament. We had a shot-gun start, so I'm just now turning."

"Does that mean you are going to be here for another hour or two—because if you are—I'd like to borrow your car for a few minutes. I need to run down to the stationery store to pick up some supplies for posters. I wouldn't be gone very long."

Tom smiled at his granddaughter, not really able to refuse her anything. "You have your license now?" he asked.

"Yep, it's brand new, but I only need to go about two miles. I'd be right back. Promise," she begged.

"I've got to hurry, baby, but here are the keys. You go check with your Dad to make sure it's okay with him. You can leave the keys at the desk here in the pro shop when you get back." He gave Sydney another squeeze and turned to go out to the golf cart to continue the round.

Sydney ran back into the office section of the building looking for her father. She heard his voice coming out of one of the offices down the hall and made a beeline for the door. Not wanting to interrupt, she stood at the door and tried in vain to get her father's attention. She really needed those supplies! He looked like he would be tied up for quite a while ...maybe she could go and be back before he finished the meeting. Against her better judgment, she decided to go ahead and drive her grandfather's car down to the store. Running quickly out to the parking lot, she spotted Tom's Escalade and hurried to the car. Sydney was absorbed in what she would need for the cheer poster for the football game Friday night, and while she drove carefully, she nudged the speedometer just slightly above the limit.

All went well until she applied the brake for the first turn. The brake pedal went completely to the floor! Shocked at the reaction of the pedal, Sydney pumped the pedal, getting nothing! She turned her attention to the vehicles in front of her, realizing that she was not going to be able to stop or even slow the heavy Cadillac. The car in front of her was beginning to slow down for the curve. "Oh God, I can't stop!" she cried. She pulled the steering wheel to the right trying to avoid crashing into the car ahead of her, but right in front of her was a telephone pole! Jerking the wheel back to the left put the car into a skid. Sydney attempted to correct the skid by spinning the wheel to the right, but being an inexperienced driver, she overcorrected. This threw the car into a roll-over, barely missing the on-coming cars.

The petite teen had buckled her seat belt, but was buffeted during the rollover. She felt her skin explode as the seat belt jerked across her chest and abdomen. Paralyzed by fear, she shut her eyes and hung onto the steering wheel with all her might, and then saw an explosion of stars when the air bag hit her, knocking her unconscious. The car slammed into a concrete abutment and came to rest upside down, with Sydney dangling from the seat belt. Blood flowed from her nose as she was hit in the face by the force of the airbag. Then all was quiet until the people in the other vehicles were able to react and come to the girl's aid. At first, no one noticed the trickle of gasoline coming from the ruptured gas tank.

*

Meanwhile, Jon had finished his meeting with Michael Stevens and began to look for his daughter. When he got to the golf shop, the pro recognized him and explained that Tom had given Sydney the keys to his car and told her to get his permission to run an errand. Jon was a bit puzzled by the fact that Sydney had not talked to him about this errand. Thinking through the situation, he swiftly walked out in the parking lot to look for his father's car. Jon's heart skipped a beat as he heard the sirens wailing in the distance. Sydney couldn't have been gone long, he thought. Those sirens just have to be a coincidence.

About that time the golf pro ran out into the parking lot.

"Jon! It's the police on the phone. There was a wreck. It's your daughter!"

Jon prayed silently as he ran to his car and tore out of the parking lot. *God please let her be alive! Please, God!*

Tom Howell was pleased with the round of golf he had just finished. He would have to wait and see how the men behind him finished, but he would post a nice solid round of 74 today. His smile didn't last long after he entered the pro shop.

"Oh, Mr. Howell, the police just called. Your granddaughter has been involved in a car accident. Jon tore out of the parking lot heading that way just a few minutes ago, and we heard sirens. It can't be very far away."

Tom was stunned as he tried to comprehend what he had just heard. Then realizing that the pro was talking about Sydney…and he had given her the keys. "I can't go to her! She was driving my car!" he cried. "Maybe Ginger is on her way over here." He pulled his cell phone from the belt holster where he carried it and quickly dialed his wife.

Ginger was on her way and would be at the club in minutes. Tom paced back and forth, his mind wildly racing about all the possibilities, but not daring to think the worst. By the time Ginger pulled up in front of the club, Tom was waiting for her at the curb by the front entry. He hopped into the car as soon as she stopped.

"Sydney borrowed my car keys," he blurted out. "She wanted to run an errand, she said. It would only be a couple of miles, she said. I told her to get permission from Jon! Gin, I may have gotten her killed! Our granddaughter!" Tom was in mental agony.

"What? Oh, no! Where..." Ginger realized that she needed to keep Tom from panic. "Just stay calm, Darling! That's a big car, and it has all the safety features. Just try to keep thinking "positive". Ginger sounded much braver than she felt. Tom pointed in the direction Sydney would have gone, and Ginger quickly headed that way.

Seconds later they pulled up to the accident scene, just as an ambulance pulled away. Several police cars and a fire truck were parked at the scene, all with lights still flashing. A policeman stopped Ginger as she approached the wrecked car. She quickly asked him, "The driver—is she alive? Where did they take her?"

"I'm pretty sure that she was alive. They are taking her down to Presbyterian Hospital Emergency." stated the patrolman.

Jon called his wife's mobile phone and told her the tragic news. Then said, "Where are you, Honey? Do you need me to come pick you up?"

"No. I am at American Furniture now. It will only take me a few minutes to get to the hospital. I'll meet you at the Emergency Room," Judith could hardly speak. She flipped the phone shut, took a deep breath, and ran out of the store.

*

While they were waiting for the doctor, one of the patrolmen came by to check on Sydney's condition. "We talked to some of the eye-witnesses to the accident. One of them said it appeared as if the young lady could not or would not slow down the vehicle, then she panicked, ran off the road, overcorrected, and rolled the vehicle. We are investigating to see if that is indeed what happened. I'd pay particular attention to the braking system when you have the body shop go over the car. By the way, this is one very lucky young lady. Gas was leaking from the tank. Any spark would have sent the vehicle up in flames. One of the firemen spotted it and sprayed the area down with foam before it could ignite." related the patrolman.

"Thanks, officer," said Tom. "We appreciate all the information we can get at this point."

"Sydney is so petite. I am sure that she would have adjusted the seat so that she could reach the brake pedal." offered Ginger. Jon nodded.

"She was very conscientious about that every time I was in the car with her. I just don't know why she took off without talking to me about it," moaned Jon.

Judith had not said a word, but silently agreed with Jon. Her face was very pale. She simply would *not* pass out, she told herself. She was holding onto Jon's hand so tightly that her knuckles had turned white.

"I guess that we'll just have to wait until we can talk to her, and maybe she can shed some light on these questions," offered Tom. His voice betrayed the fear that had taken up residence in his stomach. Sydney just *had* to wake up and be one hundred percent again or he would never forgive himself her letting her have his keys! It was almost an hour later when the doctor came out of the emergency room door to tell the waiting family the news.

"Sydney's vital signs are stable, although she has suffered a concussion or subdural hematoma, a broken nose, possible internal injuries where the air bag hit her across her chest and thighs, a broken left arm and various cuts and bruises. She is still unconscious," said the doctor. "*If* she wakes up from the concussion without a problem, then it isn't likely there will be any long lasting problems, but there are no guarantees."

***

Chapter Fifteen

Tom and Ginger collapsed onto the couch in their living room after they got home from the hospital. The emotional roller coaster was taking its toll on both of them. Maggie brought them hot coffee and some finger sandwiches, knowing that neither of them had had a chance to eat a bite. The old maid was also upset about Sydney's accident. She had babysat with Tom's granddaughter, Sydney, just as she had for his children, Jon and Leslie. The worry deepened the creases in the old woman's face. "You think Miss Sydney's gonna be all right?" she asked.

"Truthfully, Maggie, we just don't know yet," said Ginger, rubbing the back of her neck to try to relieve the tension. "She is young and healthy, which is in her favor, but we just don't know how serious the internal injuries might be. We'll just have to pray very hard for her right now. That's about all that's within our power to do to help her."

Tom closed his eyes at the thought.

Maggie nodded, and shuffled off toward the kitchen.

"We really need to call our daughter and let her know about the accident. She's too far away to come home, but she can certainly help with the praying part." suggested Ginger.

"Yes, Leslie should be made aware of what has happened to her niece." He paused, "This situation makes all of those other annoying things seem trivial, doesn't it?" said Tom, rather under his breath. "The thing that bothers me is what the patrolman said about the braking system. There hasn't been any indication of a problem with the brakes on my car, and I have it serviced regularly. First thing in the morning I'm going to call the body shop that towed if off and see if they found a problem with the brakes." He shuddered. "If that gasoline had caught fire we would be planning a funeral right now."

"Maybe we need to think about other things right now; at least until you can find out what happened. I just can't believe that Sydney was not stopping on purpose." Ginger took a sip of the hot coffee. "Can we change the subject, just for a moment?"

"I guess I should give the store some thought, even though my heart isn't in it." He paused and ran his fingers through his hair. "Did you and Cherry finish inputting the lost computer data? They hit me with the news of the accident just as I walked off the course." He had a strange look on his face as he glanced at Ginger. "I don't even know for sure who is leading the tournament, not that it matters!"

*

Meanwhile, at Rio Grande Country Club, Grant McGuire had ordered another beer. The news of Sydney's accident had raced through the club like wildfire after the police had talked to the club pro and Jon peeled out of the parking lot. If he kept drinking, then maybe he wouldn't have to think about Tom's granddaughter all banged up and in the hospital. He didn't anticipate anyone other than Tom driving his car, and had not intended for Sydney to be critically injured.

Just then Michael Stevens walked into the lounge, noticed Grant drinking alone, and came over to his table.

"Mind if I join you," he asked.

"Pull up a chair. Misery loves a guest, and you look just about as miserable as I feel," Grant replied.

"I really am not feeling anything at all," said Michael woodenly. "Nicki took my life with her when she died. I only wish I could have changed her mind. I loved her very much."

Grant raised one eyebrow. "Changed her mind about what?"

"She said she was going to talk to Tom Howell the next day. I kept trying to tell her that it wasn't a good idea. Too much at stake."

"Hmm. What do you think she wanted to talk to Tom about? What was at stake?"

Michael glanced up, thinking that he had said too much, not realizing that Grant was paying attention.

"Oh, never mind. I was just thinking out loud. I miss her very much. She just shouldn't have threatened to tell what she knew," said Michael.

The amount of beer that Grant had consumed had begun to affect his thought processes. He knew that he wasn't quite up to snuff and decided to ignore what Michael was saying, and try to talk to him about it when he was sober. "That Nicki was quite a woman, that's true," said Grant, remembering his trysts with the redhead. "You were pretty upset when she kicked you out for that snooty doctor, weren't you? But hell, everyone in town had a go with Nicki, you knew that, didn't you?"

Offended, Michael immediately stood up, knocking over his chair. "I've got to go!" he shouted at Grant, turned heel and strode purposefully out of the lounge.

*

Dr. Antonio Ciccone slipped a vial into his jacket pocket. Everyone in his office was gone for the day, and the nurse in charge of the pharmaceuticals had no idea that he knew where she kept the key to the locked cabinet. It was her responsibility to inventory and keep track of all the drugs that were dispensed, and this way, if anything disappeared, he could hold her responsible for anything that was missing. This particular drug was sometimes called the "date rape" drug. It worked like a charm. The girl that was given the drug would pass out, stay out for several minutes, depending on the amount of dosage, and would have no memory of what had taken place when she was under. She would even comply with suggestions without realizing it. Tony hadn't used it often, hadn't needed to, but he had a feeling that his date tonight might be rather difficult to get into bed. He was ready to lock the cabinet when he noticed the bottle on the shelf marked sodium pentobarbital. He remembered the redheaded bombshell, shook his head, and quickly locked the cabinet. Then he replaced the key where the nurse kept it hidden, and whistling under his breath, left the office. Just as he got to the parking lot, his pager buzzed in his pocket. He cursed as the answering service told him that one of his patients was possibly miscarrying and had been admitted to Presbyterian Emergency. He was needed immediately. *So much for my hot date tonight!* He dialed her number to cancel the evening.

*

Bud Simpson thought that he was in the clear by now. Nicki du Pree hadn't had a chance to talk to Claire. He was sure of it. And now with Nicki gone, he thought it might be a good idea to romance his wife with a little night on the town, just to keep her in line. Claire had been asking a lot of questions lately, and ever since she had taken that computer class he had kept his laptop securely locked up in the motor home, under all of the boxes that were in the top of the storage compartments, high above Claire's head. She didn't like climbing on ladders.

"Well now, Honey Bun, what would my best girl think about cuttin' a little rug t'nite with a broken down ol' cowboy?" schmoozed Bud as he pulled a bouquet of three dozen yellow roses out from behind his back and handed them to his wife.

"Oh, Bud! How beautiful! What's the occasion? And you bet, I'd love to scoot my boots with you, Sugar Pie!" gushed Claire.

"No occasion, Sweetie. I wuz just thinkin' how lucky I wuz to have a little cutie like you for my wifey! I can't stay out too late since the second round of the tournament is tomorrow, but for you, Doll-baby, I'll be willin' ta break trainin'!"

"Where do you wanna go, Baby?" asked Claire. "You know that I love to dance at the club, but I'm not sure it's gonna be much fun after what happened this afternoon."

"What happened at the club?" asked Bud.

"You didn't hear about Tom Howell's little granddaughter? She totaled his Escalade and banged herself up pretty bad. They say she's in a coma at this point."

"Is she old enough to drive? We saw her the other night at the meeting, and that little bitty girl probably couldn't see over the steering wheel of Tom's big ol' Caddy."

"The rumor was that the brakes failed or somethin' like that. Everyone's real worried 'bout her."

"That's really too bad," said Bud, "but we could still go dancin' baby. Probably have th' whole dance floor to ourselves. Whadda ya say?"

"Okay! Just let me get out of these old clothes and put on something sparkly and fun. I'll just be a few minutes." Claire ran back to the bedroom humming the latest Country and Western song, doing a little two-step as she ran.

Bud relaxed, flipped on the television and lit a cigar while he waited for Claire to change. KOAT Channel 7 News was just coming on. The lead story showed a picture of Tom's wrecked car, and the ambulance pulling away from the scene of the accident. The reporter was solemn as she said, "Eye witnesses say that the driver of the SUV may have been speeding. There was no indication brakes were applied when the vehicle approached the curve. The driver then jerked the wheel to keep from rear-ending the car in front. That driver was reported to be La Cueva High School cheerleader Sydney Howell. She was taken to Presbyterian Hospital with serious injuries. We will have more coverage on this bad accident at the ten o'clock broadcast."

Bud chewed on his cigar, thinking about the round of golf that he had played with Tom Howell. This accident must have happened just as they were finishing their round of golf this afternoon. It seemed to him that Grant McGuire had made a few disparaging remarks about Tom when he was out of earshot. "Wonder if he had anything to do with those brakes goin' bad?" he muttered under his breath.

***

Chapter Sixteen

"What!" exclaimed Tom Howell. "Are you saying that the brake line on my car had been *cut?*"

"That's right, Mr. Howell," stated the mechanic. "Even though the body was pretty well mangled with the rollover and all, it was very apparent that the line had not just busted apart. It was a nice clean even cut—all the way through the line."

"That's incredible! I can't believe that someone would intentionally cut my brake line. It's a miracle that Sydney wasn't killed, or that she didn't kill someone else! Thank God she had on her seat belt." Tom was having a hard time assimilating this new bit of information.

"Might be that you need to get the police involved, Mr. Howell. That's a pretty good case for attempted murder, if you ask me," stated the mechanic.

"Well, I want to thank you for checking the car on a Sunday morning, especially on a holiday weekend. I wasn't able to sleep after the patrolman told me that I should have you check the braking system on the car. I really do appreciate your overtime. Don't forget to put it on my bill."

"No sweat."

Tom hung up the phone, pulled out his pipe and absent-mindedly filled it with the cherry-flavored tobacco that he loved. The wheels in his mind were racing, as he tried to put this latest information into perspective. There had been no indication there was anything wrong with the brakes on his car when he parked it before the practice round yesterday afternoon. Then he came out, found the four flat tires, and called the service station to come to the club to fix them. He really hadn't checked the vehicle, except to notice that the tires were flat. He left the car in the parking lot overnight, and just glanced to see that the flat tires had been fixed when Ginger dropped him off for the first round of the tournament. Sydney took the car before he had driven it again.

Once again he blamed himself for giving her his keys, and the sick feeling returned when he thought of Sydney still in a coma. He drew a deep breath of tobacco and blew out the smoke. With the car being unattended overnight, anyone could have cut the brake line. He thought about it, then decided that perhaps it would be better to not tell Jon and Judith about the brake line, at least until Sydney woke up from the coma. They had enough to worry about.

Ginger walked into the kitchen at that moment and noticed the troubled look on Tom's face immediately.

"What is it this time, Sweetheart?" she asked as she kissed his cheek and reached for a cup and the coffee pot.

"Would you believe Sydney's accident was intentional?" he asked.

"What do you mean, *intentional?*"

"Someone cut the brake line."

"You've got to be kidding!" she spun around to face him, incredulous.

"The mechanic said the brake line had been cut."

"Oh, Tom! That means that someone was trying to kill *you*, and Sydney..." she couldn't finish the sentence.

"We've simply got to figure out who this person is, and why I am his target."

"I've been racking my brain, but for the life of me, I can't imagine who it might be," said Ginger.

"I suppose I need to talk to Pete Lucero, as this is getting pretty close to attempted murder. It's not just vandalism or pranks anymore."

"Well, so far we've been able to handle the nuisances with a minimum of trouble," said Ginger. "But now, our granddaughter is in a coma and in critical condition. And if that isn't more than enough to worry about, you've got to deal with the insurance company on your totaled vehicle, you are going to have to get a rental car just for transportation, and not only that, you're still in the middle of a golf tournament."

Tom frowned. "Well, it's simple enough to take care of *that*."

"What do you mean?"

"I'll simply call the pro shop and withdraw from the tournament. That's not a big deal at *all*." Tom tapped his pipe on the edge of the ashtray to empty the cold ashes, dug out the remainder with his pipe tool, and refilled it with fresh tobacco.

"But, you know, in the back of my mind I keep thinking that all of this harassment is targeting you just for that very reason—to get you out of the tournament—or at least distract you enough that it affects your play."

"Ginger, it's just a game! No one would go to these extremes just to win at golf."

"Who are you kidding? Some of those guys would *kill* to be able to play as well as you do, not to even mention the prestige, the amount of the prizes or the thousands of dollars in the Calcutta," stated Ginger, mentioning the auctioning of players for pretty substantial amounts of money.

"I really do find that hard to believe." snorted Tom.

"Maybe not, but I wouldn't put it past a few of those guys. For them winning is everything. Can you think of anyone that has given you a hard time about winning all the time?"

"No. Well, I'll have to give that some thought," replied Tom. "Grant grumbles about our weekly game, but that's just Grant."

Ginger finished her coffee and the rest of the breakfast that Maggie had put in front of her. "I was just on my way to the hospital to see if Judith needs me to give her a break. I doubt if she has even been home to shower or change clothes."

Just then the doorbell rang. It was their son, Jon. He looked disheveled, unshaven, and bleary-eyed.

"Jon! Come in. What's the latest on Sydney?" asked Tom.

Jon rubbed his eyes and the stubble on his chin. "No change. She's still unconscious, but her vital signs are stable. The doctor says that is good."

Ginger came over and hugged Jon tightly around the waist. "She's going to be all right, Jon, it's just a matter of time."

"I know, Mom. Believing that is all that's keeping me going right now. Judith is strong, but I don't know how long she will last without any rest. She hasn't been asleep since the accident happened."

"I plan to go see if she will let me fill in for her so she can go home for a few minutes and at least get a shower and a change of clothes," said Ginger. She looked over at Tom then back at Jon. "Jon, are you aware that your Dad is talking about withdrawing from the tournament?"

"No! Dad, you know that you shouldn't do that." argued Jon quickly. "Sydney would really be upset if she woke up and found you had quit because of her. Just go ahead and play. There is not *one thing* that you can do for her right now—or me either, for that matter. Just keep your cell phone on and we'll call you the minute there is any change. I promise." He walked over and put his arm around Tom's shoulder. "It will keep your mind occupied while we wait."

"In the back of my mind, Jon, I keep thinking all of these things that are happening to us are caused by someone who wants to prove he is better than your Dad," said Ginger. "And I agree with *you*. Maybe if Tom can go ahead and play, *and* keep his head in the game, it will flush someone out."

Jon looked puzzled. "What on earth are you talking about, Mom?"

"I guess your Dad hasn't said anything, but the list is growing. First it was the magazine subscriptions and credit card applications that we told you about. Then there was the incident with the ipecac at the club. The computers at the store crashed the next day, and Cherry found out it was an intentional virus. Then after the practice round yesterday afternoon he found his Escalade with four flat tires and not only that...."

"Ginger! That's enough." interrupted Tom.

"You may as well go ahead and tell him, Tom."

"Tell me *what?*" queried Jon.

"I wanted to wait until Sydney woke up, but I guess it doesn't make any difference. The mechanic told me this morning the brake fluid line on my car had been cut," said Tom. "And that makes Sydney's accident a possible attempted murder...only it should have been me, instead of my granddaughter."

Jon sat down without saying anything, trying to grasp this new information. "That's just incredible, Dad. Who on earth would want to kill you?"

"We don't know, son. That's why it is so frustrating. The cowardly bastard won't come forward and even tell me what his problem is. And now Sydney is in a coma, *because of me!*" Tom's shoulders slumped as he faced his son.

"You and Judith will never forgive me if Sydney doesn't make it."

"Tom!" said Ginger sharply. "Sydney is going to make it. She's going to be just fine. It's just going to take a little bit more time. We have to be patient."

"That's true, Dad. Mom is right. It is just going to take a little bit more time. And I still think that you need to go ahead and finish the golf tournament. All my life you taught me that anything you start, you finish. You need to follow your own advice."

Tom looked from one to the other. Each of them had a determined look, and Tom knew that he couldn't win the argument against this formidable duo.

"Okay, okay, okay, you win! Both of you. I'll try to win this one for Sydney. You realize, of course, that there are two more days of play, since it's the Labor Day tournament."

There was a moment of silence in the room.

"I'd like to take a shower, borrow some of your clothes, Dad, and maybe grab a couple of hours sleep before I go back to the hospital. You are so much closer here than going all the way home, and I told Judith that she could reach me here," said Jon.

"Make yourself at home, Son. You can use the Blue Room since we have Bertha and Trey staying with us for a few days in the Guest Suite," replied Ginger.

Tom looked at his watch. "You may still have time to make it to church, Ginger, if you want to go. I'll have to miss it today because of my tee time."

She turned to her husband, "I'm going to miss it myself, Tom. I'm going to the hospital to see if Judith will take a break."

"Then I'll follow you in the rental car and check in on Sydney before going to the golf course."

*

Bertha and Maggie had finished cleaning up the kitchen after breakfast, had gotten Trey busy playing with a building block set, and were sharing the Albuquerque Journal over a second cup of coffee.

"My, my," said Maggie. "Looks like a District Judge done got caught DUI! Says here he was with a woman that was not his wife, and both of them were high on cocaine. He tried to run from the cops, but they got him stopped and arrested both of them. Then he refused a breath test! My, my, what's this world comin' to! This Judge Brookmeyer is the same one that sent my cousin's nephew to the pen in Santa Fe for possession of crack cocaine."

Startled, Bertha asked, "Did you say "Brookmeyer"? I think that was one of the names Nicki mentioned to me. She overheard a couple of men talking about drugs, and that name was in the conversation. I just wish I could remember what other names she told me about," said Bertha with regret.

"Maybe it would help them find Nicki's killer. Does it mention any other names in the article?"

The two old women read through the newspaper article together, but didn't find any other names that Bertha recognized. "I'll tell Mrs. Howell about this when she comes home," said Maggie.

*

Meanwhile, Ginger convinced Judith to go home to rest for a while. While sitting with Sydney, she read the article about Judge Brookmeyer. Brookmeyer had been arrested for DUI, and it specifically mentioned cocaine. She briefly wondered if it could be related to the conversation Nicki overheard. She shook her head at the lack of honor this man had exhibited for his high office in the legal profession.

She then turned to the sports section and read through the story about the golf tournament at Rio Grande Country Club and found that Tom was leading in the first flight by three strokes over Bud Simpson and Grant McGuire, who were tied in second place. Dr. Ciccone was five strokes back of Tom.

***

In Total Darkness

Chapter Seventeen

After the visit to the hospital Tom Howell was still very worried about Sydney. *Even though the prognosis sounds good, she is still in a coma. Maybe tomorrow she will be awake and can talk to me about the accident if it doesn't upset her too much.*

Right now, however, he had to get a mind-set to play tournament golf. He went through his usual routine of hitting balls on the practice range to warm up, hit a few out of a bunker, chipped a dozen or so balls, and then went to the putting green. He would be paired today with the same three men that played with him in the practice round: McGuire, Ciccone, and Simpson.

"Well. Tom, are you ready for me to outscore you today for the first time in my life?" laughed McGuire.

"I'll believe it when I see it, Grant," Tom retorted good-naturedly.

"Would you like to make a little bet with me, McGuire?" asked Bud Simpson. "And how about you other guys?"

"Not me," answered Ciccone. "I want to concentrate on my golf swing."

"I make it a practice to not make bets during tournament competition, Bud," replied Tom.

"How about you, McGuire? Want to put your money where your mouth is?"

"No. Ciccone has the right idea—concentrate on the swing."

There was an incident on the very first hole. After each of the four men teed off, Grant McGuire drove his cart up beside the shortest ball, paused to look at it, then drove over and parked beside the next ball over in the fairway. Bud Simpson then drove to the shorter ball, got out of his cart and hit his second shot.

"Sorry, Bud, that's a two-stroke penalty. You just hit my ball." cried Grant.

"What? You drove up and looked at this one and drove away. What do you mean, I hit your ball?" replied Bud, frowning.

"Just what I said. You hit my ball. This one is yours," Grant said, smugly pointing to the ball where he was parked.

"Of all the dirty..." started Bud.

"Yeah, Grant, what's that all about?" asked Tom.

"Rules are rules. He should have identified his ball."

"That's true, but then why did you look at it and pull away, like it wasn't yours!" cried Bud.

"Hey, all's fair in love and war, and golf," said Grant, with a crooked smile. "I just went into second place all by myself."

The group was rather subdued after the incident. Bud seethed with anger, and watched Grant very carefully to see if he could catch *him* violating a rule.

*

When Jon and Judith returned to the hospital, Ginger left them and went out to the club for lunch. She sat down at a table that had a view of the 18th green, so she could watch Tom's foursome finish their round.

"Good afternoon, Mrs. Howell. Ready for some lunch?" asked Paula, the waitress.

"Yes, Paula, and I don't need a menu. Just bring me the Turky-Lurky—half-order, and my usual can of Dr Pepper. And of course the glass of ice and some maraschino cherries, please."

"Mind if I join you?" said Pamela Johnson as she walked up to Ginger's table.

"By all means, Pamela, be my guest." Ginger pointed to an empty chair.

"Just bring me the other half of Ginger's Turky-Lurky, Paula, but I'll have Scotch on the rocks instead of Dr Pepper."

"And what is your member number, Mrs. Johnson?" asked Paula. Pamela responded and sat down with a thump.

"Whew, what a day!" said Pamela.

"Rough one, huh?" asked Ginger.

"There was a dog show at the Fairgrounds, and I have to stay sober enough to be able to run my little Yorkies around in that big circle. I guess I shouldn't complain as that's about the only exercise I get," she laughed.

"I'll bet that's a lot of fun. I have a little Yorkie, too, but he had progressive retinal atrophy at birth, and now that he's older he has cataracts in both eyes. He could never have been a show dog, but we don't tell him he can't see. It's amazing how well Scooter functions without sight. We really love the little guy," said Ginger. "He is *such* a personality!"

"My dogs are my babies, too, and since I don't have children, they are very precious to me. That's why I'm still mourning my little Penelope Queen." Tears filled Pamela's eyes. "I had to put her to sleep."

"Oh, that's too bad. Did you have another vet do that for you since your husband, Arnold, is gone?"

"Actually, I gave her the shot myself. I still have the drugs that Arnold kept in his office, and I assisted him many times."

"You still have drugs? That's a bit surprising, isn't it? Don't you use sodium pentobarbital when an animal is put down?"

"That's right. I keep all the drugs locked up in Arnold's office, right where he left them. I might not have been able to do it with as much as I had to drink that day, but a nice man from the club made sure that I got home and helped me fix the syringe."

Curious, Ginger asked, "Really? Who was that?"

"You know, I didn't even get his name? I have seen him here at the club a few times lately, though. I need to thank him again."

A thought just occurred to Ginger. "Pamela, did Pete Lucero talk to you about those drugs you have?"

"Oh, yes," she replied. "A nice young man came with him. He poured the coffee for me," she smiled at the thought of Patrick's help.

"Did you tell him about the man that helped you with Penelope Queen?"

"I don't remember, but I don't think I mentioned him," Pamela frowned trying to think.

"If you see that man around here, would you point him out to me, please? It might be very important."

"Sure. Be glad to. Oh, here's our lunch," said Pamela as she spotted Paula coming from the kitchen with a tray. "I am *really ready* for that Scotch!"

By the time Pamela and Ginger finished their lunches, Tom's foursome had finished the eighteenth hole, checked and signed their scorecards and turned them in. Then they went by the locker room to freshen up.

Bud Simpson was still miffed about the dirty trick that Grant had played on him, and didn't mind saying so.

"If we are never again paired up with each other it would suit me just fine," he spouted at Grant.

"Don't be such a spoil sport, Bud. Look at the valuable lesson you learned—never hit a ball until you identify it as your own," laughed Grant.

"Well, it wasn't a very gentlemanly thing to do, Grant, regardless of the rules of golf," disapproved Tom.

Dr. Ciccone just shook his head and didn't respond. He had not scored well, and was trying to think about his golf game and what to do to correct his mistakes.

"They should have the scores posted by now, so let's go take a look and see how we stand." suggested Tom. "Someone in another foursome may have left us in the dust for all we know."

When they got down to the patio where the scores were being posted, the golf pro was just writing down the last score. Tom was still in first place, but Grant had moved up to within one shot, Bud had dropped back another shot and was now four behind Tom, and Tony was a distant seven shots back. The rest of the field was not in contention.

"Looks like we'll have a real shoot-out tomorrow, doesn't it, Tom," said Grant.

"So what's new? We go head-to-head every Wednesday," responded Tom.

"That's right. And I have yet to even tie you, much less beat you…ever! But tomorrow may be a different story, huh, Tom."

"Well, I hope that we both play our best game, and may the best man win," he smiled at Grant. "Sort of like the old days at college, Grant."

"My day is coming." stated Grant firmly. Tom did not see the look on Grant's face when he made this last statement. His eyes narrowed, his mouth was set in a tight straight line, and his fists were clenched.

When Tom and Grant walked into the lounge, Pamela took one look at Grant and leaned over to whisper in Ginger's ear. "That is the nice young man that helped me get home, the day I had to put Penelope Queen down." She nodded toward Grant.

"Are you sure, Pamela?" asked Ginger quietly.

"I am absolutely certain of it. Even when I'm full of Scotch I would recognize that face."

Grant waved at Ginger and proceeded into the men's card room while Tom joined the ladies.

After a cordial greeting, Pamela excused herself leaving Tom and Ginger by themselves.

"Any news about Sydney?" were the first words out of Tom's mouth when he walked over to join Ginger.

Ginger shook her head, "No word, but then sometimes no news is better news, Sweetheart." She took a sip of her Dr Pepper.

"Looks like I'm going to have to send you to Dr Pepper Anonymous, if you keep this up," said Tom, waving his hand at the two empty cans on the table.

"It does look like I surpassed my limit, doesn't it?" smiled Ginger. "How did you play, today?"

"Not as well as yesterday," replied Tom. "However, neither did anyone else. I am still leading the flight by one stroke over Grant." He frowned. "Grant didn't make any points with Bud Simpson today, that's for sure." He then told Ginger about the incident on the first hole.

"That was a pretty dirty little trick," responded Ginger.

"Something else happened, but I can't prove it, so it just seemed to be the better part of valor to keep my mouth shut."

"What was that?"

"Grant sliced a ball out into the rough off the tee box on number eleven, you know, out into that dead grass area? We weren't in the same cart, and I had walked over to hit my second shot on the left side of the fairway. He looked for his ball for several minutes and hadn't found it yet. I am sure Bud was timing the search, after the incident on number one. You are aware that you only have five minutes to search for a lost ball when it is your turn to hit. Anyway, I was heading over to help him look when he called out that he had found it. I was certain that he had a second ball in his front pocket, but when he got back to the cart, that second ball was gone."

"So you think he dropped the second ball out of his pocket and claimed it was the lost one, so he wouldn't have to take a penalty?"

"I think so. That doesn't say much for the character of my good friend, does it?"

"Poor Grant. His life is such a mess. What he needs is a good woman."

"He hasn't had much luck there, either," remarked Tom. "But enough about Grant! How do you think it's working out with our house guests, Bertha and Trey?"

"They seem to be about as happy as they could be, under the circumstances. I know that Trey misses his mommy, but he seems to be coping okay for a little guy."

"I think so, too. Well, let's go by the hospital to check on Sydney, then by the store to make sure everything is locked up tight for the weekend and to check our messages. I'll be glad for this tournament to be over tomorrow."

"Do you know your tee time, yet?" asked Ginger as they stood up to leave.

"It's the last one of the day, as they like the first flight leaders to come in after everyone else is finished," replied Tom.

*

Michael Stevens, the Rio Grande Country Club assistant manager, was extremely busy with all of the activities associated with the Labor Day Golf Tournament. The General Manager had been on his case all day about the organizational details involved with all of the extra meals, drinks, and service personnel. During a five minute break, Michael finally had a chance to catch his breath. His thoughts always turned to his beautiful Nicki. He had considered talking to the Homicide Detective about the conversation Nicki overheard and although she had not told him the names of the men, she had mentioned the topic of their conversation and described the two men to him. It just might be important in trying to find out who had killed his lover. Michael resolved to call Pete Lucero as soon as he had some free time.

***

Chapter Eighteen

Pete Lucero and Patrick Mahoney were reading through the list of names for the fourth time.

"We've been over and over these names. Are you getting any kind of ideas at all about where we need to go next with this investigation?" asked Patrick.

"We've pretty much eliminated Michael Stevens, unless we can make some connection between him and the sodium pento-stuff," said Pete. Dr. Cocon..uh..Ciccone is hot on two or three counts: he could get the stuff and would know how to use it, he had intimate ties with Nicki, and he was in the building. Then there's Bud Simpson, who fits at least two of those same criteria.

"I ran into an interesting fact about Bud Simpson on Dora this morning," said Patrick, using his favorite nickname for his computer. "It seems that he is registered as a lobbyist in Santa Fe. He represents some of the Native American tribes on their gambling issues."

"Well," replied Pete, "I don't know how that might apply to this current case, but then you never know. Speaking of his criteria, he might have an "in" on the drug. Guess we ought to check with his vet, what do you think about that? If the vet was pretty careful about the drug, then Simpson might have a hard time getting it. Also, we haven't yet talked to this Grant McGuire person that Simpson told us about," said Pete.

"That's correct. Maybe we should have a visit with Mr. McGuire. I'll give him a call."

*

Grant McGuire wasn't too happy about the trip downtown to talk to the homicide detectives, but he figured that they would eventually get around to him, so he wasn't surprised. It would cut into the time he needed to set up Tom's next little "surprise," however. This one should put old Tom right on his heels. He felt badly that the granddaughter was injured, but maybe that was the way to get to Tom…through his loved ones, he thought.

*

"So, Mr. McGuire, you know why we have asked you to come down to the station?" asked Patrick.

Grant smiled, "My best guess would be that it has something to do with Nicolette du Pree."

"Good guess," said Lucero. "How would you describe your relationship with Nicki?"

"She was one hot little number. I like hot ladies…a lot!"

"So you slept with her?"

"Many times."

"And when did these little sleep-overs take place?" asked Pete.

"Off and on during the whole time she worked at the club," responded Grant, smugly.

"Even when she had other men living in her home?" asked Patrick, rather shocked.

"That didn't seem to be a problem with Nicki, and it certainly wasn't a problem for me. A night with Nicki was like having a hot fudge sundae…pure decadent delight!"

"Was that all she meant to you—just one-night stands?"

"Nicki was looking for security—equating to wealth. My finances are a wreck, right now, so even if I *had* wanted to make a long-range plan with Nicki, I knew that I'd never be able to keep her, so I just settled for whatever I could get."

"Mr. McGuire, do you use recreational drugs? You know, of course, that we could probably figure out a way to do a drug test on you," bluffed Pete.

"I don't think my attorney would allow that to happen."

"We have information that you might have been supplying Nicki with her cocaine," offered Patrick.

"You don't really expect me to reply to that statement, do you?" asked Grant. "I thought you homicide cops were smarter than that."

"Let me put that another way, Mr. McGuire. We *will* find out where Nicki got her cocaine, and we *will* find out if it was you. It might go a little easier for you if you cooperated with our investigation."

"Oh, really?" said Grant sarcastically.

"Believe it! We are not charging you with anything—at least not yet," said Pete. "But that can change any time we find incriminating evidence against you."

Grant narrowed his eyes, deep in thought. He was weighing the consequences of telling these guys about his cocaine use, and whether they could in any way tie him into dealing. "If I know the law, you haven't read me any rights, so anything that I say right now could not necessarily be used against me. Also, I think that you could not arrest me if I said that I used cocaine unless you caught me in the act. Is that correct?"

"Right now Mr. McGuire we are more interested in a murder investigation than in nailing someone for recreational drug use. Would you like to answer the question now?"

Grant pursed his lips, and then sneered, "Okay, so I occasionally use cocaine. So what?"

"Did you ever supply Nicki with cocaine for her use?"

"No, I did not."

"Where do you get the cocaine that you use? Would you like to give us a name?" asked Patrick.

"You've got to be kidding! No way. I'm really not ready to die, and if I give that kind of information to you, I'm dead meat."

"Do you have access to a drug called sodium pentobarbital?"

"Sodium pentobarbital?" he innocently asked. "I've never heard of it. Is it an upper or a downer?"

"Never mind. I don't think that we have any more questions for you right now, but we would like for you to be available if other questions come up. In other words, we would prefer that you not leave town."

"That's not a problem. I'm not planning on any trips in the near future," replied Grant as he rose and left the office.

"What an asshole!" exclaimed Pete, as soon as Grant was out of earshot. "I'd really like to find *something* with which to charge that dude."

"Not a very pleasant guy, that's for sure," said Patrick.

*

The meeting with Lucero and Mahoney had upset Grant more than he was willing to admit. The question about the sodium pentobarbital was unexpected. He remembered that Pamela Johnson had asked him to help her the day she had to put down her dog. She asked him to get a bottle of that drug out of the pharmaceutical cabinet in her husband's vet clinic. Of course she was too drunk to realize that he had helped himself to a couple of other items at the same time. He hoped that these homicide detectives would not be able to figure out that he had access to the drugs at Pamela's house. He looked quickly at his watch and then hurried out to his car. He didn't think there would be time to set up Tom's "surprise" tonight. It just might have to wait until after the tournament. He would just have to keep reminding Tom of Sydney. That might be enough of a distraction to keep him out of his game. Then tomorrow night for sure!

*

Maggie and Bertha were waiting for Ginger when she and Tom finally got home, and while Tom headed straight for the shower, Ginger stopped to talk. "What's going on, gals?" she asked the two older women.

"We've been waiting for you. Bertha remembered one of the names that Nicki told her about when she overheard those men talking. His name was in the paper. It was Judge Brookmeyer!" cried Maggie.

"Brookmeyer? The one that was arrested for DUI? Bertha, do you remember what Nicki said about the judge?"

"I do remember. Nicki told me the man said that Judge Brookmeyer was needing some more "stuff" and that he was one of their best customers, so they didn't want to keep him waiting."

"But Judge Brookmeyer wasn't one of the men?"

"No, the two men were just talking *about* him."

"Do you remember any other names, Bertha?" asked Ginger.

"I've tried and tried, but I didn't remember this one until I heard Maggie say the name. Maybe if I heard the names, then I'd remember if that was someone Nicki mentioned."

"Since this Brookmeyer has been arrested, he might be willing to make a deal to provide the cops with other names to make it easier on him, especially since the woman he had in his car wasn't his wife," mused Ginger. "I'll pass this information on to Pete Lucero first thing in the morning."

*

Early the next morning, Tom brought in the Albuquerque Journal that had been delivered to their front door. The headline jumped out at him when he unfolded the paper: JUDGE BROOKMEYER COMMITS SUICIDE. Tom was still reading the story when Ginger came into the kitchen for breakfast.

"Oh, no! Judge Brookmeyer is dead? Tom! The two men that Nicki overheard were talking about him. Bertha said that Judge Brookmeyer needed some more "stuff". I presume they meant drugs. I was going to call Pete Lucero this morning to let him know. I thought he might be able to make some kind of deal to get information, since the Judge was arrested for DUI. What did the paper say happened and how could he commit suicide while he was in jail?"

"The Judge had to remain in jail until he could locate his lawyer and have him arrange for a bondsman to bail him out. I guess that took too long. He hung himself. They found him hanging in his cell late last night, according to the newspaper."

"Do you think there could be any connection between this judge and what happened to Nicki?"

"I have no idea, but it would not surprise me at all." Tom ran his fingers through his hair. "In fact, his death may have been murder, not suicide. These people seem to play for keeps!"

***

Chapter Nineteen

"Pete, this is Ginger Howell."

"Hi, Ginger. What's happening with the Howell family today?"

"I just called to tell you that Nicolette du Pree's nanny read in the paper about Judge Brookmeyer's being arrested. It jogged her memory, and she told us that Nicki said the two men she overheard were talking about Judge Brookmeyer needing some more "stuff".

"No kidding!" Pete had started using Patrick's favorite expression lately.

"She didn't come up with any more names. I should have gone ahead and called you last night when she mentioned it to us, but I thought I could wait until morning. Judge Brookmeyer might have been able to give you lots of information and names connected to Nicki's murder. I couldn't believe it when I read in the paper this morning that he was dead."

"I was quite surprised by the suicide of Judge Brookmeyer, but I am shocked that there might be a connection to Nicki's murder. Thanks a lot for the information. If the nanny remembers anything else be sure to give me a call. By the way, how is that granddaughter of yours?"

"There's been no change yet, unfortunately. Pete, we'll call you if Bertha remembers anything else."

*

"Looks like we are going to have to broaden our investigation, Patrick. This puts a whole other slant to things, doesn't it?"

"If the Judge's source got worried about him cutting a deal for information, the "suicide" might have been "helped along".

"This case gets more "squirrelly" by the moment, Pat, my boy."

"No kidding!" Patrick responded with his favorite expression. He had been saying it a lot lately. "How about this scenario? Judge is buying drugs from the same dealer that is selling to Nicolette du Pree. Judge gets caught, not only DUI, but with another woman that's not his wife. Judge decides that a bargain is the best way for him to get off with the lightest sentence as he doesn't have a prayer to survive if he goes to jail. Meanwhile, the dealer, who has pretty powerful ties, decides that the judge is now a liability, arranges for a couple of guards to dispatch the judge and make it look like suicide," postulated Patrick.

"As far-fetched as that sounds, it might even be plausible," responded Pete. "Think that the lab boys can tell the difference if he staged his own hanging or if someone else did?"

"If I remember correctly, this judge wasn't that old, and was a pretty good-sized man. They would have to subdue him in some way, even if there were two of them."

"This might open up a whole box of Pandoras," exclaimed Pete.

"Open up what?" asked Patrick.

"Never mind. It's just an expression that a former governor of ours used to say." Pete took a big swig of the thick, evil-tasting, liquid—otherwise known as coffee, and asked, "What else do we have on the agenda for today?"

"You know, of course, that today is a holiday for all the government offices. For one thing, we might check with the veterinarian that Bud Simpson uses, to see if he can account for all of his sodium pentobarbital."

"You think that vets close on Labor Day?" He paused and scratched the stubble on his chin. "Why don't you call the vet. I might just make a phone call to Ricky the Rat—see what might be shaking on the drug scene."

*

Labor Day was a favorite holiday for Albuquerque people. It was the last gasp of summer, and the last chance to take a three-day weekend holiday before the kids started back to school. Everyone wanted to be outside in the warm sunshine, to have the last swimming party for the year, to spread picnics under the shade trees, or just to enjoy being with the family. At Rio Grande Country Club, the final day of the golf tournament brought all of the families of the participants out to the club for the barbeque, swimming, and to watch the golf.

Tom and Ginger had spent most of the morning at the hospital with Sydney. She was still unresponsive. When he got ready to leave her room, Tom bent down, kissed Sydney on the forehead and whispered to her, "I've got to go now, Sweetheart, but I'm going to play this round just for you. I can't wait for you to wake up so I can tell you all about it." Tears welled up in Ginger's eyes as she heard what Tom said.

On the way out, Ginger said, "I have a good feeling about today, Tom. This just might be the day that Sydney comes out of the coma."

*

Out on the driving range, Tom, Grant, and Bud were warming up. Bud refused to speak to Grant, and moved over several spaces so that he would not have to watch him swing. Grant seemed edgy. Tom was focusing on his practice swing.

"Well, looks like this is it, old buddy." chirped Grant. "Winner takes all."

Tom looked at Grant, did not reply, and teed up his next shot.

"What's the matter, old buddy? A bit tense, are you? Can't speak to me anymore?"

"Knock it off, Grant. This is a golf *game*. It's just a game. I'm here to try to play my best, and I assume that you will do the same. I suggest that you don't try to pull any more of those tricks you used yesterday on Bud. He's about ready to take you over into a sand trap and use a wedge on you."

"No sweat. I can handle Bud." Grant glanced over at Bud, started to say something, but changed his mind and started trying to concentrate on hitting the ball.

The first four holes were uneventful. Tom, Bud, and Grant all had pars, so the standings remained the same. Tom had a par on the next hole, while Grant bogeyed, and Bud had a chip-in eagle, bringing him up even with Grant. They both were now two strokes behind Tom. They all three had bogeys on the sixth hole, and each of them had pars on seven, eight, and nine.

Ginger met Tom when he pulled in to make the turn. "Any word on Sydney?" asked Tom, as soon as he saw Ginger.

She shook her head, then asked, "How's it going?"

"Not much change. I think that Bud and Grant are now tied for second, and I have a two shot lead on the two of them. Only nine more holes to go and we can forget about this tournament."

"Keep up the good work, Hon. I'll be right here when you finish," said Ginger.

*

The standings remained unchanged until the fifteenth hole. Just as Tom started his downswing with his driver, Grant dropped his metal club onto the cart path, making a horrible clanking noise. Startled, Tom missed his drive, dribbling the ball just off the end of the tee box. He turned to see what happened.

Grant shrugged his shoulders, and with both palms up, said, "Sorry 'bout that. I dropped my club."

Tom did not respond to the comment, but ended up with a bogey on that hole. This brought Bud and Grant both back within one shot of the lead, as they both had a par.

On the next hole, Grant started up the gas golf cart to move it, just as Tom started the downswing for his second shot. Startled once more, Tom again missed the shot, and bogeyed the sixteenth hole. However, Grant shanked his approach shot and also bogeyed. Bud had a birdie, putting him into the lead by a shot over Tom, and two shots over Grant.

The seventeenth hole was a disaster for Bud. His tee shot went out of bounds, costing him one stroke and distance, the next shot went into a lateral water hazard, also costing him a shot. He was out of contention with a triple bogey. In the meantime, Grant got lucky with a chip shot and made a birdie, to Tom's par, putting them into a tie for the lead.

On the eighteenth and last hole Grant was so nervous he could barely hold onto his club, but took a deep breath and managed a decent drive. Tom's drive was long and right down the middle. Approaching the green on the par four hole, Grant put his second shot right in the middle of the green, about twelve feet from the hole. Tom's shot was a bit short, landing in the throat and running up to a position on the first cut around the green, about thirty feet from the hole. Taking dead aim, Tom used a putter and ran his putt to within a six inch tap in for a par.

All Grant had to do was to make his twelve foot putt to win the championship. He looked at the hole from all four sides, knelt down to check for a break, hung his putter down to plumb-bob, and finally took his stance to putt. Drawing back his putter, he decelerated the stroke and hit his ball about halfway to the hole. Now he had to make this putt to tie. He was almost hyperventilating from the tension. Taking aim again, he stroked the putt nice and firmly right at the cup. Thinking that it was in all the way, he smiled broadly and stooped over to take his ball out of the hole. However, the ball hit the edge of the cup, did a perfect horseshoe around the lip of the cup and came to rest about two inches from the hole. Grant fell to his knees, cursing. Tom Howell had won the tournament—again!

"You were robbed," said Tom sympathetically, as he reached out to shake Grant's hand.

Grant couldn't trust himself to speak. He did manage to shake Tom's hand and then headed straight for the bar.

"Congratulations, Sweetheart. You did it again!" cried Ginger as she joined Tom walking back to the clubhouse.

"I'm not sure old Grant is ever going to be the same. I thought he was going to pass out before he hit that last putt. Poor guy. He wanted to win so badly." said Tom. "Now I just want to go see Sydney, then go home and collapse. All the stress of the past few days has about given me an ulcer."

*

When they got to the hospital, Tom went in to give Sydney a kiss.

"We did it, Syd. Just for you. When you wake up, I'll tell you all about it." whispered Tom into her ear.

"Since you have the rental car and I have my car here Tom, why don't you go on home? Judith looks like she is about to crater. I'm going to see if she will let me stay with Syd, so she can go home for a few hours."

"I'm out of here, then," said Tom as he left.

Turning to Judith, she said, "Okay with you?"

"I am about to crash and burn, Ginger. I would appreciate it if you will stay with Syd while I go home and clean up. I can be back in an hour or so," replied Judith.

"It's a holiday; our store is closed along with the post office and government offices. There isn't a thing that I had rather do than sit with my granddaughter. You take your time. I'll be here as long as you need me to be."

Ginger settled into the visitor's chair beside Sydney's bed, opened the newspaper and started working the crossword puzzle of the day. She hummed softly while she concentrated on the words. The afternoon was quiet, and after a couple of hours, Ginger dozed off.

"Nonnie?" came a small little voice from the hospital bed.

Ginger bolted out of the chair and leaned over her granddaughter. "Syd?"

Sydney's eyes were open, but cloudy with the painkillers that she had been given.

Ginger pushed the button for the nurse to come, and gently squeezed the delicate little hand. "Yes, Sydney, it's Nonnie. I'm right here, Baby. Don't try to move. You have a concussion and a broken arm, but you're going to be all right."

"What happened?" she mumbled.

"Don't worry about anything right now. Try to relax. You had an accident. No one else was injured. Are you in pain right now?"

"Everything's a little fuzzy. I don't feel much of anything. What's this tape across my nose?" She looked cross-eyed at the bandage that was holding her broken nose in place.

Just then the nurse responded to the call button.

"Well, well, look who is back to the land of the awake and living!" said the nurse brightly. "I'm going to call the doctor that is on call to take a look at you now that you can speak to him."

While the doctor examined Sydney, Ginger took the time to step out into the hall and place a call on her cell phone to Tom.

"Tom, Sydney just woke up! The doctor is in with her right now. Isn't that wonderful?"

"Thank God! Is she talking yet?"

"Yes! I had dozed off, and she woke me up when she called my name. I won't know anything further until the doctor gets finished with his examination."

"Is Judith still there with you?"

"No. I was going to call her as soon as we hang up. I just

wanted you to know. Sydney is still groggy from the drugs, of course. What do you think? Should I call the kids or wait until the doctor comes out?"

"Why don't you talk to the doctor after he examines her, then you will have something to report. Maggie said that Jon left here about an hour before I got home and was going to check on a construction site on his way back to the hospital."

"Oh, the doctor is coming out now. I am *so relieved!* I'll call you back after I talk to him."

The doctor's report was very encouraging. All of the exterior injuries were healing nicely, although she had two black eyes from the broken nose and the other bruises had turned black. Her broken left arm was splinted and in a temporary cast. The doctor felt that the concussion would take some time and bed-rest, but barring unseen complications the prognosis was promising.

Ginger called Jon's cell phone to tell him the good news.

"That's wonderful! Judith and I will round up Brandon and "J". They will want to see their sister. We should be back to the hospital in a half-hour." Everyone breathed a big sigh of relief.

***

Chapter Twenty

The family stayed in Sydney's hospital room until the nurses finally ran everyone out. It was then decided to celebrate Syd's awakening and Tom's victory with a big dinner.

*

Maggie outdid herself, with chicken-fried steak, mashed potatoes and gravy, green beans, a tossed salad, iced tea, and a great big chocolate cake. The house was noisy and happy with the sounds of a family dinner. Relief permeated the atmosphere.

Finally, it was quiet. Jon and his family had gone home; Jon had called his sister, Leslie, to tell her the good news; Maggie and Bertha had finished cleaning the kitchen and put Trey to bed. Tom and Ginger went directly to bed, as well. Soon, the only noise in the entire compound was the sound of the old grandfather clock, busy ticking its way toward midnight.

Ringgg! Ringgg! When the telephone rang it startled Ginger out of her deep sleep. She reached for the bedside phone and sleepily answered it.

"This is the Security Company. We have an alarm going off at a location on Comanche close to I-25," said the toneless voice.

"Whaaat?" questioned Ginger, trying to wake up and comprehend what she was hearing.

"This is the Security Company. We have an alarm going off at…"

"I heard you! I heard you!" interrupted Ginger. "What kind

of alarm is it?"

"Fire, ma'am. The code says there is a fire at that location."

"Fire? Have you called the fire department?"

"Yes, ma'am. Both the City and the County units have responded. Ginger slammed down the phone and threw off the covers.

"Tom, the store is on fire!"

Tom and Ginger were both wide awake by now and scrambling to get into street clothes so they could race down to the carpet store to see what was happening.

Tom felt as if he had been punched in the stomach. The pumper-trucks from the fire department were already in place, pumping thousands of gallons of water on the metal roof of the building. Smoke was billowing from the end of the warehouse that was on the opposite end of the building from the showroom and offices. As soon as Tom and Ginger got out of the car, they were stopped by a fireman, who would not let anyone approach the building.

"But I'm the owner of the store!" cried Tom. "I have a key to the front door, in case they need to enter the building!"

"Sorry, sir. You can't get any closer. It is for your own protection."

The water being pumped onto the metal roof was not hitting any part of the fire but simply running off into the paved parking lot.

"I don't understand!" cried Ginger. "They aren't putting water on the fire! It's just running off into the street!"

"It has to do with combustion, ma'am," said the fireman. "If they open those doors and oxygen hits the flames, it's much worse."

"But everything inside is burning!" protested Ginger.

"Sorry, ma'am. I'm just following orders. We have to protect lives more than property."

Meanwhile Tom and Ginger watched helplessly as the amber glow of the fire kept creeping toward the offices, and the thick, black, smoke curled up in a plume toward the sky. A

In Total Darkness

loud explosion pierced the noise of the activity around the burning building. Tom and Ginger glanced at one another.

"That was the propane tank on the fork lift," said Tom. He grimaced as the acid in his stomach took its toll.

"They aren't going to be able to stop it!" cried Ginger. "The whole place is going to burn to the ground." Tears started streaming down her cheeks. They continued to watch in disbelief.

After a while, a hole finally burned through the metal roof, allowing water to pour into the building and onto the fire itself.

"I have the key to the front door. If they will let me go unlock it, the firemen can go in that way," said Tom to the fireman.

Just about that time, one of the firemen from one of the units swung an axe, breaking through the glass double doors into the front of the store.

"That was an eight hundred dollar door that they just smashed," said Tom flatly. "I could have opened it. There's no fire at the front of the building right now."

Ginger felt sick to her stomach, watching the years of hard work and long hours go up in smoke. A large number of people had gathered at the perimeter of the area, watching the building burn.

"How could this have happened, Tom? There isn't anything flammable at that end of the warehouse. Do you think it could have been an electrical short?" asked Ginger.

"Other than the overhead lights, there isn't anything *electrical* back in that area, either, Gin. I think that it has to be arson. Somebody set that fire," he agonized. Ginger gasped and buried her face in her hands.

One of the men standing nearby was a truck driver that had parked his rig in front of the business across the street, waiting to make an early morning delivery. He turned to Tom and said, "I wonder if this fire has anything to do with a white pickup truck that came tearing around the corner about midnight. After I saw him, smoke was coming from the building. Seemed pretty coincidental to me."

"You saw someone driving away from this building, in a big hurry?" asked Tom. "What kind of vehicle was it?"

"White Ford crew cab pickup with duallies, pretty new, maybe a couple of years old. I thought he was going to hit my trailer, so I tried to get a license plate. I have a delivery for Nobel-Cisco, the grocery people across the street, and I pulled over there to sleep until morning. I wanted to be first to unload in the morning."

"Would you be willing to tell the police what you have just told us?" asked Ginger.

"Well, yeah, but I've got a schedule to run and I'll have to be out of here as soon as they unload my trailer," he said.

"What is your name, and the name of the company that you drive for?" asked Tom. "And what was that license plate number?"

"I only got the first three letters. Didn't get the rest of it."

Tom jotted down the names and letters and tucked it into his shirt pocket. Meanwhile the fire had advanced all the way through the warehouse and was now burning into the two-story bank of offices. When the roof collapsed, the water began to hit the blaze, and finally put it out. The fire had been extinguished before it burned the bookkeeping and executives offices.

"We may be able to salvage some of the furniture that didn't burn, Gin, but the building is a total loss," said Tom.

"Surely we can rebuild on the existing concrete slab. I can't imagine that the fire would damage that," replied Ginger.

*

It was late the next afternoon before the fire department allowed anyone to enter the building. Thick black smoke had settled on and covered everything that had not burned. The interior of the building had an eerie quietness as Tom and Ginger carefully made their way through the showroom.

"Don't touch anything, Tom, or you'll have black soot all

over you," cautioned Ginger. "Our footprints are in the smoke."

They made their way up the stairs and into the bookkeeping department. If the door to the kitchen had been closed, the executive offices and bookkeeping would have been spared most of the smoke damage. The desks and computers were not burned, but were completely enveloped in the fine, choking, smelly, soot that had settled into every nook and cranny.

"You know, I think I'll call Harris, the computer technician to see if any of our computers are salvageable. We'll need him to see if we can get the company data up and running again. As luck would have it, I took the backups of the main frame out of the store with me when I left last Friday. All of the data should still be intact." murmured Ginger.

"Look, Gin, the fire stopped at the kitchen. These metal desks aren't damaged, just covered with smoke. They can be cleaned. We'll take them down to the house and use the studio for temporary offices."

"Tom, that's a great idea!" Ginger tried to keep positive.

"I talked to all of the salespersons this morning. We'll move them all down to our outlet store. They should be able to operate out of the Carpet for Cash store without any problems. I notified them to call all of their customers that were expecting installations today and find out if they want to come down and pick out a replacement or wait for a reorder."

*

"Mrs. Howell, I don't think that the computers were actually damaged—just smoky," said Harris, the computer technician. "I think that I can take them apart, clean all of the components and re-assemble them."

"That's wonderful, Harris. How much time do you think it will take?"

"I should be able to have four or five of them back up and running by tomorrow afternoon."

"I'm amazed. Go ahead and get started as soon as you can.

If we don't have to buy all new equipment immediately, it will certainly be helpful."

"Well, I don't think they were affected by the smoke, but I will need to load all the programs and the data from your tape back-ups just to be sure."

True to his word, Harris had all of the computers cleaned of the smoke, tested, and reloaded with the company data by the next afternoon. They worked just fine.

*

The huge rolls of carpet that were stored in the warehouse smoldered for three days, often breaking out in flames again. Each time, the fire department had to come back and wet them down again. Finally, the fire chief gave the word that it was safe to load the burned rolls of carpet onto a trailer to take to the land fill area. The fire department then brought in equipment to scrape off the concrete slab. Once the concrete foundation was cleared, the fire chief found the fluorescence that is always there when an accelerant is used to start a fire. It was definitely arson.

***

Chapter Twenty-One

Grant McGuire drove past the store the day after the fire.
"That ought to slow Tom Howell down a bit," he murmured to himself as he surveyed the charred wreckage of the building. "Now let's see how Mr. Perfect handles *this* mess!"

*

"What do you think, Ginger, should we just close the business, collect the insurance, and retire?" Tom's face showed the stress of all that had happened.

Ginger looked up quickly, took Tom's hand and said, "I think that the time to get out is when we're at the top. When we are *up, not down!*"

Tom pulled his wife into his arms, stroked her cheek, and smiled, "You are right, of course. We couldn't do that to our employees, and it wouldn't be good for us, either. We'll work our way through this mess, just like we always do."

"It's not going to be easy, you know that. But we can make it just fine—one day at a time."

The next few weeks were a blur of activity for both Tom and Ginger. They had to meet with the insurance adjuster, make provisions for warehousing new carpet that had been ordered, and lease a truck for transporting rolls of carpet to the

Carpet for Cash store to be cut and picked up by installation crews. The business of the store continued as if there had been no fire. Thanks to Harris, the computer technician, the bookkeeping staff had been able to create invoices the second day after the fire. But even as business continued, the air everywhere was permeated with the stench of acrid smoke. Hands were washed twenty times a day, and invariably the smudges of smoke ended up on cheeks and noses as well as hands.

The insurance company hired "clean-up" crews to start cleaning the smoke off the documents that needed to be saved. They used treated sponges to wipe both sides of each sheet of paper which removed most of the smoke.

All of the women on the bookkeeping staff pitched in to clean the desks and the rest of the office furniture and equipment. They also had to clean their personal items that had been left at the store and were now covered with soot.

"I don't think my hands will ever be the same," moaned Cherry, the head bookkeeper.

"It wouldn't be so bad, if everything just didn't *stink* so badly," said Janette.

"Well, it certainly has helped to have that ozone machine in here every night." replied Cherry.

The ozone machine was brought into the building the first night the desks were moved into the studio at the Howell Estate. It ran all night, but for health reasons, had to be turned off before the girls got to work every morning. It left the air in the building smelling like the forest after a refreshing rain, but through the day, the odor of the smoke again filled the room with the stench. For Ginger it was déjà vu. Her family home burned to the ground when she was still a teenager—not long after her father died. The smell of the parched papers that had been salvaged brought back all of the old haunting memories from her youth. It took all of her courage to simply "go to work" every morning and to face that smell.

After an initial meeting with the insurance adjuster, Tom spent a lot of his time trying to get a true assessment of the actual financial loss. He made arrangements with the insurance people to continue with payroll for all of the employees so they would not suffer financial loss because of the fire. He discovered very quickly that insurance was certainly not going to cover all of the losses incurred.

"I am not sure at all that the figures we have discussed will cover our losses, but I presume that we may adjust that figure as the need arises? Tom questioned the adjuster.

"We like to get a pretty definite estimate in to the home office as quickly as possible, but there is no set deadline."

"By the way, we had an interesting incident happen the night of the fire. This truck driver was standing there where Ginger and I were watching the building burn. He made a comment about seeing a pickup leaving the area at high speed just before he saw the smoke coming from the building."

"That is interesting information. Could he give you any other description—of the driver or the pickup?"

"He thought the driver might be going to hit his rig, so he made a point of trying to get the license plate. He did manage to get a partial. Here are the first three letters. He didn't get the rest of it." Tom also gave the adjuster the description of the Ford pickup the driver had related.

"We'll turn this information over to our investigator. Maybe he can turn something up with it."

After a week of recovering from the shock of the loss of the store, Tom and Ginger settled into a "normal" pattern in the abnormal situation.

"We had some really good news today, Sweetheart," said Ginger.

"Please tell me. I could stand to have a bit of good news for a change," replied Tom.

"Jon called me this afternoon. They released Sydney from the hospital today. Isn't that wonderful?"

"That's great! It was such a relief when she woke up. But I won't be happy until she is totally back to normal," said Tom.

"She won't be fulfilling any of her cheerleading duties right away, with that cast on her arm, and I'm sure that she will be sore for a few more weeks. However, she's upbeat and sounds like her old self again, according to Jon. And, she doesn't have a pair of black eyes anymore."

"I still want to talk to her about the accident, but it can wait. I strongly suspect that whoever cut the brake line on my car also set the fire at the store," said Tom, as he popped another antacid tablet into his mouth.

"How about we take a break tomorrow and go out to Rio Grande Country Club for lunch?" said Ginger. "It just might help to shake the cobwebs out. I think that all of the salespeople have been great about contacting their customers, and the staff seems to be adjusting to the new situation with a minimum of difficulty. I don't think they would miss us for a couple of hours."

"Good idea. I'll clear my calendar and we'll go out about eleven-thirty to miss the noon traffic." He looked over at his wife and said, "You know, don't you, that if I didn't have you I would have collected the insurance check and just shut the business down?" The kiss that followed said more than any words Ginger could have replied to Tom's statement.

***

Chapter Twenty-Two

Tom and Ginger quickly settled into the routine of putting their business back in order. It was a little different to just walk out the back door of the home and into the studio office with eleven desks, and the entire bookkeeping staff. Ginger's dog, Scooter, loved it! He could hardly wait for Ginger to be dressed and to "take him to work" with her. As soon as they would enter the studio/office, Scooter would immediately go to each one of the girl's desks as if to check and make sure they had come to work that day. He quickly became the store mascot.

"Hi, Scooter!" cried Cherry, the head bookkeeper. "How's our little guy today?" She reached down and gave him a scratch behind his ears. Scooter licked her hand and proceeded to the next desk.

"Cherry, as soon as things are going smoothly here I am going to the office building and make a mail run," said Ginger.

"Okay, we'll keep it going here." she replied. "How is it working out with those new tenants?" she asked.

"Oh. You mean Ava Grissom and the Saudi Arabian Bank of Belgium—and her favorite "bodyguard", Alfred Benedetti?"

"Yeah. Those are the ones."

"That remains to be seen, Cherry. It's a little doubtful at this point."

*

Ginger walked into Tom's office to let him know where she was going, then added, "You know, Tom, with all that's happened lately, I forgot to tell you something. I talked to the banker the other day. The check that Ava Grissom gave us for the lease payment on the office building still has not cleared. He told me that a check on a foreign bank had to go through an international clearinghouse, and that he had sent it to Chase Manhattan. It's been three or four weeks. I would have thought it would clear by now."

"Huh." Tom looked up from the reports that he had been studying. "Well, Babe, don't be a bit surprised if you finally find out that it isn't going to clear at all. You probably need to think about an eviction notice if she can't come up with another source of payment."

"Another thing I've noticed since I have been delivering mail to the offices in the building—there seems to be a lot of second notice type of billings going to Ava's office—you know—the ones with the pink invoices showing through the windows? It's almost as if she isn't paying anyone—for anything."

"Well, you might be correct there, too," replied Tom. "Let's just keep an eye on that situation for another week or so, and if nothing is resolved we'll worry about her then."

"She did hire a receptionist/secretary-type person. I can't imagine that Alfred or this girl is working gratis." Ginger took a deep breath and exhaled it slowly. "You know, I'm really ready for some *normal* living again, aren't you?"

Tom glanced up at his wife. "You bet I am. It's almost as if everything that can go wrong has gone wrong lately—including Nicki's murder. But I can handle the harassment and all the rest of it as long as you are here beside me."

Ginger reached over and patted Tom's hand. "Thanks. And you know I'll always be right here." She turned to go, then stopped in the doorway. "I wonder if there are any new developments in Nicki's case."

Tom shook his head.

"I also wonder who the devil has so much time on his hands he gets his jollies in harassing you."

"I know. I really can't imagine who it might be."

"I just wish we could catch the stupid guy who thinks it is so much fun to wreck our lives," replied Ginger.

"Sooner or later he's going to make a mistake, and then we'll catch him."

"Have you talked to Pete Lucero lately?"

"Not in several days. I may need to check in with him. The insurance investigator was going to talk to him about everything that has been happening. As far as Nicki's case, I think it would help tremendously if Bertha could just remember the conversation Nicki discussed with her."

"You are right about that. I've gotta run. Catch you later."

*

In the meantime, Grant McGuire was enjoying watching his best friend suffer. He knew that it had caused him a lot of grief, but it didn't appear that Tom Howell was totally stressed out or ready to have a break down or anything like that. Grant had thought that by now Tom would be ready to throw in the towel, but he just kept working his way out of the mess. He took another big swig from the can of beer—and noticed that there were already four empty ones in front of him. He frowned, drained the can he was holding and headed to the refrigerator to get another. *What was it going to take for this guy to crater?* He frowned again as he opened the last can in the six-pack and let the darkness settle into his brain as the cold brew settled into his stomach.

*

Dr. Antonio Ciccone looked out his office window at the golden leaves falling from the cottonwood trees, and sighed. He was staying busy with his practice in obstetrics and gynecology during the day, but his nights had never been the same since he had moved out of Nicki's house. He never dreamed that a little redheaded cocktail waitress could make such a difference in his life. He had been with several women since Nicki, but none of them could light his fire the way Nicki had. She made him feel so alive—like every fiber of his being was tingling. He was devastated when she asked him to move out.

Most of the women in his life were simply a physical release for him—he couldn't even get interested in pursuing that nurse up on the fourth floor of the hospital that was such a challenge for him. Other women seemed to always be ready, willing, and able to try a relationship with him, but *that* nurse didn't give him the time of day, and because of Nicki, he didn't really care. Hmm. He looked at his polished fingernails and sighed again. *Almost sounds like clinical depression*, he thought.

*

Bud Simpson had decided to take his wife, Claire, on a three-week cruise to the Caribbean before the holiday rush began. He thought that it might take her mind off this computer class she was taking. It scared him to think that she would learn how to get into his laptop and pull up some of the information he kept there.

"Hey Claire, what would you say about th' two of us gettin' in a little extra sunshine?"

"Oooh, that sounds wonderful! Maybe somewhere there's a big ocean and a beach and everything." Claire loved the idea.

"Well, I wuz kinda thinkin' the Bahamas. Whadda say?"

"I *love* the Bahamas! Remember the last time we were in Nassau? Those guys dived right in the water and brought up the conch shells." She shivered in delight. "Then they told us that the locals *eat those things.* They pull the critters right out of the shells and throw the shells right back in the water."

"I figger we would be home in plenty of time for Thanksgiving. It always gets a bit hectic with the holidays, and then the New Mexico legislative session begins in January."

"This is the perfect time to go, Sugar. Can I go start packing?"

"Well, you know how the first two months of the year are the busiest time of the year for the lobbying business. I have to be gone so much when the Merry Roundhouse goes into session that this will give me some special time alone with my favorite little gal."

He always took the motor home to Santa Fe and stayed there while he was lobbying the congressmen. This meant that he didn't have to spend two to three hours a day driving back and forth from Albuquerque to Santa Fe.

*

Pete Lucero was perplexed about the progress in the du Pree murder investigation. Not only that, his personal life was in a mess and he missed his wife and kids. He and Pete, Jr. used to love the fall. They couldn't wait for the World Series to start, and they usually found time to play some catch on the weekends. And his little daughter, Rosie—what a sweetheart. He smiled as he thought of the way she would cock her head to one side and put on this really big smile when she wanted something from him, and he could never tell her "no". He sat slumped down in his office chair, chewing on a pencil. He had read about depression, but refused to think that he, of all people, would actually be depressed. Carmen just didn't understand the time pressure on a homicide detective.

Patrick Mahoney tapped on the frame of his open door.
"Hi, Pete. Got a minute?" he asked.
"Huh? Oh, yeah. I've got all the time in the world—NOT. I keep going round and round with all the loose ends in the du Pree case, for one thing."

"That's what I wanted to talk to you about. I know that the fire at the Howell business has been on everyone's mind, and even though it doesn't appear to be related, maybe it is."

"Related? How?"

"You know that I keep a notebook on everything? I was going back through it the other day, and it just seems that Tom Howell's name kept popping up every few pages."

"You aren't saying that Tom Howell is involved in Nicki's murder?" asked Pete. "That's preposterous!"

"No, no. Of course not. But there are all of these items in my notebook. We talked to Michael Stevens about the night Nicki was killed. When he was recounting the evening, he mentioned that Tom Howell was supposed to give a speech, but someone had slipped ipecac into his coffee, making him sick to his stomach. Ginger had to give the speech."

"Yeah, so what?"

"Could have been a diversion—from what was taking place in the ladies locker room." Patrick looked down at his notebook again.

"Then we get a call from Tom about the letter that Nicki had mailed to him before she died, and he suggested that we check out her house. However, there didn't seem to be anything in the house that was a clue to her murder."

"Right. The house was clean. Nothing to tie Nicki to drugs or anything else out of the ordinary that we saw.'

"Then there was a call from him about attempted murder. First, all four tires were slashed on his car and then the brake line was cut. The granddaughter drove the car, wrecked it and was almost killed when the brakes failed."

"So either Tom Howell is a real coincidental victim of vandalism, or someone is out to get him. Is that what you are saying?"

"Not yet. The next incident was the supposed suicide of Judge Brookmeyer. Again, the Howell's were in the notebook, because the nanny recognized Brookmeyer as one name that

Nicki overheard and mentioned to her. Then Mrs. Howell called to let us know."

"Didn't we follow up on that?"

"I don't think we did."

"Why not?" asked Pete.

"Just haven't gotten to it yet. Then there was the arson. Somebody torched Howell's business. Tom called to tell us about the truck driver that saw the pickup speeding away from his building just before the smoke started pouring from it."

"Yeah, well, arson doesn't necessarily tie into murder."

"Maybe not. Maybe so. He gave the information on the pickup to the arson investigator as well. Arson investigators are working on the partial license plate. What I am seeing here is a pattern. Someone is definitely out to get Tom Howell, and the tie-in to the murder case is the letter that he received from the victim. We just don't know what that tie-in is yet. We need to talk to this nanny again, we need to take a look at Judge Brookmeyer's autopsy report, and we need to try one more time to follow up on the sodium pentobarbital."

"Patrick, my boy, you sure do know how to take my mind off my problems, don't you? Carmen would be proud of you." Pete got a far-away look on his face every time he spoke about his estranged wife. "Speaking of Carmen, do you think that I ought to call her and ask her out to dinner?"

"Why not? If she says "no" you won't be any worse off than you are now, right?"

"Well, why don't you write that down in that notebook of yours, Patrick? Have Pete call Carmen. Got it?"

Patrick smiled, and wrote the memo into his notebook.

***

In Total Darkness

Chapter Twenty-Three

Patrick looked at the list, picked up the phone and called the Howell Estate telephone number.

"Howell residence, this is Maggie," she said answering the phone.

"This is Homicide Detective Patrick Mahoney. Would it be possible for Homicide Detective Lucero and me to come to the house and speak to Bertha?"

"That would be just fine. We have no plans to leave the house this morning," answered Maggie.

Sitting out on the patio with a freshly brewed cup of Maggie's coffee, Lucero and Mahoney enjoyed the beautiful view of Sandia Peak across the newly cut field of alfalfa. This would probably be the last cutting of the season. In the distance, the neighbor's hay barn was stacked to the top with bales of green hay. Cows grazed along the banks of the irrigation ditch, completing the quiet pastoral scene.

"It is so peaceful down here," remarked Patrick.

"Sure is," replied Pete. "One could almost forget all of the crime that is going on in the city."

The youngster, Trey, was kicking a football as he ran across the lawn in the back yard.

"How is the little boy adjusting to life without his mother," asked Patrick.

"He cries for her at night, but during the day he stays busy--and Nicki was gone a lot. He is a happy little boy for the most part," replied Bertha.

"We still have not been able to contact any other family. There is a good possibility that Nicki's parents have passed away, and there doesn't seem to be any other next of kin," commented Pete.

"Oh, I should have told you. There are no other relatives." She glanced fondly at the little tyke. "He has a home with me for as long as I live," said Bertha. "I don't know how long the Howell family will allow me to stay here, but we'll find someplace. I was going through some of Nicki's papers and discovered that she had set up a trust account for Trey before her husband spent all of her money. It's a large sum of money. More than enough to take care of the two of us until Trey is out of high school, maybe even college."

"I hate to bring this up again, as I know it is upsetting to have to think about Nicki, but we need to ask you if you have remembered anything else she might have told you about the two men she overheard talking?"

"I have gone over and over the conversation, and it seems to me that Nicki mentioned saying something about these two men to Mike Stevens. Even though he wasn't living with us anymore, she seemed to still think a lot of him, and she may have confided in him at work,"

"It's strange that he would not have mentioned it when we questioned him, if she had said something about it. Tom Howell said that she seemed to be pretty upset when she called him the night she was killed. However, Stevens was very distraught about Nicki's death, so he may not have been thinking about those two men," offered Pete.

"I did remember that she sort of described the men to me. One was pretty tall, had a mustache and I think she said he had dark hair, and that he was pretty big."

"By big, do you think she meant "fat" or just strong-looking?" asked Patrick.

"I don't know." Bertha closed her eyes tightly as if trying hard to remember. "I got the impression she was talking about "muscled" as if he worked out a lot."

"What about the other man? Did she say anything about him?"

"She called him a "typical politician-type". He apparently had a mustache, too, and she said that he was pretty short and sort of round."

"Anything else?"

"Not that I can remember, right now. Just that the two men were concerned about getting a delivery to Judge Brookmeyer, because he was such a good customer."

"Thanks, Bertha, maybe there *is* something here that we can follow up on, and get closer to finding Nicki's killer," said Pete.

"In the meantime, I still think that you should stay pretty close to home. We don't want these two men to find you and bother you."

*

As the two detectives left the valley estate, they rehashed the conversation with Bertha.

"Two things," said Patrick, "that we can follow up on. We need to check with Stevens again to see if he remembers Nicki saying anything about these two men."

"What else?" asked Pete.

"I think that I can use Dora, my computer, to pull up newspaper clippings of the state congressmen and just check them over for physical characteristics. We might not be able to pinpoint an exact person, but we could make a list of "possibles"."

"Okay. However, a short, round man with a mustache, and a typical politician-type—what the heck is that?"

"I can think of several congressmen right now that would fit that description. It's going to be interesting to see how that plays out."

"Okay. You go talk to Dora, and see what that little computer spits out. I'll take a drive out to Rio Grande Country Club and see if Mike Stevens remembers anything that might give us a clue."

"Fine. You can drop me off at the office and be on your way. Call me when you're on the way back and we'll plan on some lunch."

*

Pete was in luck. Mike Stevens was in his office, and could see him immediately.

"How are you doing, Mr. Stevens?" asked Pete, in a concerned tone of voice.

Mike sighed. "Well, I can honestly say that I am better today than I was when I talked to you in your office a few weeks ago. I guess time does sort of take a little bit of edge off the pain, but not much. I still can't believe that she is gone."

"Patrick and I were just talking to Nicki's nanny, Bertha. You know her, of course, since you lived in Nicki's house for a time."

"Of course. How is Trey getting along? He is such a cute little kid. Spitting image of his mom."

"Oh, he's fine. You know how kids are. Pretty resilient. The reason I wanted to talk with you has to do with a conversation that Nicki overheard here at the club. She told Bertha about these two men who were talking about drugs, for one thing, and about Judge Brookmeyer being one of their best customers."

"Yes. She mentioned it briefly to me, as well. I was really too distraught at the time we talked, or I would have mentioned it."

"Please tell me all that you can remember about what Nicki told you."

"Just that these two men seemed to be connected with drug dealing."

"Did you see them?"

"No, I didn't. It was the morning before the big dinner

dance, and I had my hands full of the preparations for the evening. I really didn't pay much attention to what she said about them."

"Did she describe them to you?"

Mike smiled wryly. "I think she used the term "slugs" when she mentioned them. Let's see. She might have said that one of them was a member here, and the other man was a state senator or congressman."

"She didn't mention the member by name?"

"No, she didn't. I'm sure I would have remembered if she had."

"This question might be painful for you, but I need to ask it, anyway. Paula gave us the names of two other men that were in a relationship with Nicki—Bud Simpson and Dr. Antonio Coco—uh-Ciccone. Were you aware of any others?"

"Yes. Grant McGuire for one. He told me as much the other day. He indicated that Nicki had slept around with a lot of different men, but he didn't mention any other names. I was still pretty upset at the time, and didn't appreciate his insensitive comments."

"We are aware of McGuire's connection with her." Pete stood up, ending the conversation. "If there is anything else you remember about the two men Nicki mentioned to you, please call me. It might be important."

"Of course. I'll be happy to do anything I can to help find her killer."

*

Upstairs in the lounge, Tom sipped on a cup of coffee as he waited for Ginger to meet him for lunch.

"Mind if I join you?" asked Grant McGuire. He motioned for a waitress and ordered a beer.

"Be my guest," said Tom, indicating a chair. "Did you just get off the course? I thought maybe you had sworn off playing after the pressure of the Labor Day Tournament."

Grant grimaced. "Oh well. You know what they say about

getting back on a horse that's bucked you off! And yeah, I just tackled the course, the wind, and my horrible slice, all in one four hour round. I'm exhausted."

"It does look a bit breezy out there," Tom glanced out the window at the flag on the eighteenth hole. "Would you say about twenty-five miles per hour breezy?"

"Maybe. It felt more like fifty!" Grant drained the first can of beer and ordered another one. The two men chatted comfortably for a few minutes, then Grant said, "I really was sorry to hear about your building burning down, Tom," he lied. "That's really got to be a tough pill to swallow, after all your hard work."

"To tell you the truth, it hasn't been easy. What really makes it worse is to know that someone would go to those lengths to harass me. The fire chief is certain that it was arson, but of course you already knew that, since it was in the newspaper."

"Yes, I did read about it. I can just imagine how upsetting it is. Did you see it burn, or just find out about it after the fact?" Grant watched Tom's face carefully, hoping to see the stress.

"Oh yes, the company that monitors the alarm system called us and told us the building was on fire. Not a very pleasant wake-up call to get in the middle of the night. When Ginger and I got there it was fully engulfed in flames, but only at the back of the warehouse. Then we watched as the fire worked its way toward the offices. The Fire Department got it stopped when a hole finally burned through the roof so the water could hit the flames. The warehouse and the entire inventory are a complete loss, as well as the kitchen, the decorating studio, and the warehouse office. We were able to salvage all of the desks and computers out of the bookkeeping office and my office and Ginger's were spared—except for the smoke."

"That's a lucky break. Did any of your employees quit?"

"Oh no. The staff has been wonderful. They have all worked their tails off, getting everything up and running again. We didn't lose our computer data, as Ginger had the backup disc in her purse that she made on Friday night. We didn't even miss any installations."

"Really? That's amazing. How on earth did that happen?" Grant hid his disappointment.

"All of the salespeople called the customers that were expecting an installation the next day and had them come down to the Carpet for Cash location to reselect their carpet. Only one or two decided to wait on a reorder."

"The stress of all of this has got to be getting to you, doesn't it? Especially after what you went through with your granddaughter's wreck."

"It has been stressful. Especially when I think Sydney could have been killed when someone intentionally cut the brake line on my car. Not only that, but there have been a lot of other incidents."

"Oh, really? Someone actually cut the brake line?" Grant was a master at sounding so concerned, when he was actually enjoying hearing Tom talk about the problems that *he* had created. "What kind of incidents?"

"Nothing that I want to go into right now, but I will tell you this: I would never have been able to survive all of this if I hadn't had Ginger by my side! Having Sydney almost killed was a horrible experience. I felt so guilty, giving her my keys. I don't know if I would have been able to stand it, if it had not been for Gin." Tom stopped and sipped his coffee. "Ginger is my life."

"She's quite a lady, all right," said Grant, looking at his watch. "I've gotta go. I'm meeting a business associate in about fifteen minutes, and I can just make it, if I hurry. See you later, old buddy." Tom didn't see the look on Grant's face as he left the room. Another dark idea was forming in his mind.

*

When Pete Lucero left Mike Stevens' office he almost collided with Ginger Howell. She was headed up to the lounge area to meet Tom for lunch.

"Whoa. Almost ran over you," said Ginger. "What brings you out to this neighborhood, Pete? Is it an official visit?" asked Ginger.

"Still trying to connect the dots," he smiled.

"Why don't you come up and join us for lunch. We just have to get away from the smell of smoke every once in a while."

"Sure, why not?" responded Pete. "I'll just call Patrick and tell him that I just got a better offer."

The trio exchanged small talk while their lunch was being served, and then the conversation headed back to Nicki.

"Any progress in finding Nicki's killer, Pete?" asked Tom.

"Slow and steady. Patrick was just commenting on how many times your name has come up in his notebook during this investigation. We'd really like to find this guy that has it in for you, Tom."

"So would we!" exclaimed Ginger.

"I did hear your granddaughter was out of the hospital."

"Yes, she is. It's amazing how well the young can bounce back from something like that," said Tom.

"Speaking of bouncing back, you two have done an amazing job of bouncing back from that arson," said Pete. "I haven't had any information from the investigator that he has found the arsonist."

"So there are no arrests, yet?" questioned Ginger. Pete shook his head.

"What's your next move?" asked Tom.

"We're going to look over the autopsy report on Judge Brookmeyer. Patrick has this hair-brained notion it might not have been a suicide."

"Murder? While he was in a jail cell? How could that happen?"

"Bribery. It's just speculation at this point, but a guard could have his back turned while a couple of goons enter a cell and stage a hanging. Make it look just like he did it himself."

"But wouldn't the guard get caught?"

"Possibly, but maybe not if the hanging looked enough like suicide."

"Wow. This thing is growing bigger by the day. Like it had a life of its own." exclaimed Ginger.

"Brookmeyer was connected to the two men that Nicki overheard talking, and she gets killed, then the judge gets caught DUI and he's dead. One more thing came out this morning when I talked to Bertha again."

"What was that," asked Tom.

"It seems that Nicki told her that one of the men was a member of this club, and the other was a politician. I don't know how many people know where Bertha is staying, but that little old lady might still be in danger."

"We have tried to keep it quiet. None of us have said anything to anyone about Bertha and Trey being at our house. I'm sure of that," said Ginger vehemently.

"Hmm. Wonder who that club member could be?" muttered Tom.

"We still have Bud Simpson, Dr. Cocon…uh..Ciccone, and Grant McGuire that might be connected to Nicki."

"Grant? He used to be my college roommate. I'm sure he probably put a move on Nicki, and he's a sort of loose cannon, but he's still a good friend, and I think he's pretty harmless," said Tom.

"Well, I'm not so sure about that, Tom, and maybe you are right, Pete. I think he should be questioned," commented Ginger.

"I wasn't very impressed with him when we talked to him downtown," said Pete. "Are you aware that he's been using cocaine?"

"Really?" Tom was shocked. "He's had a rough go with his businesses and his personal relationships, but I didn't realize he was a drug user."

"Speaking of drugs," interjected Ginger, "have you discovered where the sodium pentobarbital was acquired?"

"According to Patrick, that's next on the list of items we still need to investigate. We talked to Pamela Johnson…"

"Pamela!" cried Ginger. "I knew there was something I had been meaning to tell you, Pete. The day of the golf tournament I had lunch with Pamela. She said she had gotten pretty drunk the day she had to put down her dog, Penelope Queen. I guess she started drinking here at the club, and that some "nice young man" helped her get home and with the euthanasia. When Tom and Grant finished their round, they came up here and Pamela pointed out Grant as the man that helped her home that day."

"That means he would have had access to the old vet's medicine cabinet, if he helped Pamela with the dog," surmised Pete.

"That's possible," said Tom, "but I still can't believe Grant would be involved in murder."

The three of them sat without talking for a few minutes, as each of them sorted out the information they had shared.

"Well, Pete, Tom and I need to get back to the smoke pit. I'd like to say that it was really a pleasure to visit with you, but…."

"I know, I know. As usual, though, you two have given me some new ideas about how we can proceed on this case." He turned to Tom and said, "Please try to stay out of harm's way, old buddy. We have enough on our plate right now down at our office."

"I'd like just five minutes with the turkey that thinks making my life a wreck is so much fun." replied Tom vehemently.

Tom and Ginger lingered over dessert and coffee awhile after Pete left them.

"I went to the bank this morning," began Ginger, "and you'll never guess what they told me."

"Good news, I hope?"

"Not exactly. Ava's check bounced. Not only did it bounce, it was written on a non-existent bank."

"Well, that doesn't really surprise me. I thought there was something fishy about her from the beginning," stated Tom.

"I'm going up there this afternoon and confront her with this news, and will probably give her an eviction notice."

"Need some help?"

"I don't think so, but I'm not really fond of her bodyguard, Big Al..."

"Big Al?"

"Alfred Benedetti. You know who he is—Ava's goon."

Tom laughed. "Where in the world did you pick up such language? I think you've been watching too much television lately."

"I wish! I'd gladly trade working with smoky documents with a little quality television."

Tom took her hand and said, "It certainly hasn't been easy, has it Sweetheart?"

"I'm not really complaining. We'll just take one problem at a time and we'll be just fine." A sparkle came into her brown eyes and they crinkled up at the corners when she smiled and said, "I was going to say that we could just put out one fire at a time, but it sounded sort of corny, under the circumstances!"

***

In Total Darkness

Chapter Twenty-Four

Patrick was waiting for Pete when he got back to the office.
"What's up?" asked Pete.
"I just finished talking to the coroner about Judge Brookmeyer's autopsy. It looks like my hypothesis may have been closer to the truth than we thought," responded Patrick.
Pete looked up quickly, "Are you serious?"
"He found residue of tape on Brookmeyer's wrists, and marks showing that his hands were probably taped behind his back. It would be very difficult for him to hang himself under those circumstances," said Patrick with a wink.
"Puts a whole other spin on things, doesn't it," mused Pete.
"I interviewed the guard on duty that night, when we first learned about the "suicide". He told me another guard came up to his station and said the head of jail security wanted to see him down in his office. When he got downstairs, the head guy wasn't in his office. He waited for him a few minutes, checked the john and the cafeteria, but couldn't find him. He was gone about fifteen or twenty minutes in all."
"What about this other guard?" asked Pete.
"He didn't recognize him, and thought he might be a new employee. When he got back upstairs this "new" guard was gone and the post was vacant. Then he got concerned and started making the rounds to check on the prisoners. That's when he discovered Brookmeyer."

"So what did the head of jail security say about this new employee?"

"They didn't have any new employees. The guard was so upset about Brookmeyer he was scared to death to tell them he had left his post, so he just didn't tell them. He figured it was bad enough that Brookmeyer committed suicide on his watch and he was already in trouble."

"So someone dresses up like a guard, gets the one on duty away from his post, maybe he has a helper waiting in the wings, they do Brookmeyer and make it look like suicide and split before the guard gets back. Amazing!" said Pete.

"Chavez has worked for Bernalillo County Detention Center for fifteen years, and the poor guy will probably get canned."

"If Brookmeyer was that deep into drugs, no telling who else is involved. He might have been a real gold mine of information. No wonder they wanted him dead!" exclaimed Pete. "Seems to me we're dealing with some pretty heavy hitters here, and it's probably the same person that killed Nicolette du Pree."

"Wait a minute. If I remember correctly Brookmeyer had a woman with him when he was arrested—a woman who was not his wife. She might have been with him when he bought the drugs they were using."

"Good thinking, Pat. Check it out. See if they arrested her as well. She might be still in the pokey."

"I'll do that right away." He started to punch in the telephone number, then asked, "What did you find out from your talk with Mike Stevens?" asked Patrick.

"Not much we didn't already know. Nicki did mention overhearing the conversation to him, and he remembered Brookmeyer's name, but not any other names. She did tell him that one of the men was a member of the club, and the other was a politician."

"Line is busy. I'll get back to them later." Patrick turned to Pete and asked, "A member of the club and a politician?"

"Yes—which confirms what Bertha had to say."

"So now we have two lists—the membership roll at Rio Grande Country Club and the New Mexico state legislature. That's quite a list of suspects," stated Patrick.

"Something else I haven't told you yet."

"What's that?"

"We can now put Grant McGuire on the list of people with access to that sodium pento-stuff."

"Mike Stevens told you that?"

"Pamela Johnson, our little Scotch-drinking lady, mentioned it to Ginger Howell. Pamela got drunk at the club and Grant McGuire helped her get home—and to put down an old dog. He had access to that drug cabinet."

"No kidding!"

*

Ginger took a deep breath and walked into the office of the non-existent Saudi Arabian Bank of Belgium.

"May I help you," asked the mousy little receptionist.

"I would like to see Ava Grissom. Is she in?" replied Ginger.

"Just a moment, please. I'll check and see if she is available. What is your name?" She took a slip of paper and wrote Ginger's name down as if she might forget it, scratched her head, and pushed her glasses back up on her nose, then pushed the button on the intercom to announce Ginger's presence.

"Ms. Grissom, there is a Gin—ger How—ell to see you. Shall I send her in?"

"Ginger Howell? Of course. Send her right in," replied Ava.

"Ginger. How nice to see you. Please have a seat," said Ava enthusiastically, as Ginger came into her office.

"I'm afraid my visit is business, Ava," said Ginger. As she sat down, she glanced around the tastefully decorated room. Ava sat behind a large, ornate, executive desk. Her burgundy chair sat on a six-inch high platform, allowing the rather short woman to look down upon her guests. To the side was a circular glass topped conference table with four white upholstered chairs. The base of the table was made up of three brass elephants, their trunks high in the air, upon which rested the glass top. A large vase full of silk lilies sat majestically in the middle of the table. Several framed prints of the Master's artwork hung on the walls. To the other side of Ava's desk in a comfortable-looking chair sat Alfred Benedetti.

"What kind of business did you wish to discuss, Ginger?" asked Ava. "Would you and Tom like to take out a loan? I read about the fire. Will your insurance take care of replacement?"

Ginger glanced over at Benedetti, who was staring at her, then back at Ava. "No, Ava. My visit has nothing to do with a loan. It has to do with the check that you gave me for the lease payment on this office. It was returned. Chase Manhattan returned it to our bank, finally, and said that the Saudi Arabian Bank of Belgium was non-existent."

"That has to be a mistake," said Ava calmly. "We run into this all the time when dealing with international banking. I realize that the temporary check that I wrote you must have been cause for concern, but now I have official checks from the bank. Would you like for me to replace that original check?"

"I would really like for you to give me a money order or a certified check that I can cash immediately," replied Ginger. "It has taken way too much time trying to clear a check on an international bank, especially one that does not exist."

"I assure you, Ginger, the bank *does* exist. If you will allow me to write you a new check today, I will get in touch with the sheik and see how quickly we can arrange cash payment. How does that sound?" Ava took out a checkbook and busily began writing a new check. She was very professional sounding, and did not seem upset at all about Ginger's charges.

"Under the circumstances, Ava, all I can promise you is that you may have until the end of the week. If this new check won't clear by then, eviction proceedings will start."

Benedetti shifted in his chair and glared at Ginger, but said nothing.

"Don't worry about a thing, Ginger. I will take care of everything!" said Ava.

When Ginger left Ava's office, Alfred Benedetti waited a minute or so, and then followed her. Watching her descend the stairs, he flipped open his cell phone and made a phone call.

***

In Total Darkness

Chapter Twenty-Five

Dr. Antonio Ciccone had all the symptoms of classical depression. He was lethargic, had no appetite, couldn't sleep, and had a total lack of concentration. He knew what was wrong, but did not want to admit it, even to himself. He had lost the love of his life. Nicolette du Pree was the first woman he had ever met that really took his breath away. He had never been happier than the few weeks he had spent living with her— and he had never been as miserable as when she asked him to leave.

He was certain that the sodium pentobarbital that had killed Nicki had not come from his office, but he had a sneaking suspicion of where someone might get it. Ricky the Rat knew everyone, and he would know where that drug was available. If he could help the homicide detectives find that source, then maybe they would scratch him from their suspect list. He picked up the phone and dialed the number he had memorized.

"H'lo," was the furtive answer.

"I have a deal for you," said Ciccone, without identifying himself.

"Wha' kinda deal you talkin' 'bout?"

"Could be worth a thousand bucks."

"Talk to me, man."

"I need to find out who has been buying a drug called sodium pentobarbital," replied the doctor, "without a prescription."

"Sodium P, huh? Who do I call when I find out?"

"You don't call me. I'll call you tomorrow, and if your information is valid, the thousand will be with the bartender at the Silver Eagle Bar, got that?"

"Got it," replied Ricky the Rat.

The doctor hung up and sat back in his office chair with his face in his hands. He was feeling pretty guilty about the way his life was going. It had been a real kick, having his fling with all the women, but after Nicki he realized just how much he was missing in life by not having an honest relationship with a woman he really loved. Maybe he could make amends by helping find out who killed Nicki.

*

Grant McGuire was still stewing about the conversation that he had with Tom Howell at the club. Even with all the stuff he had thrown at him, Tom bounced back like a cat with nine lives. He downed the last swallow of beer in the fourth can. Tom always had Ginger to back him up. *What if Ginger wasn't there for him?* A devious plan began to form in his alcohol-soused brain.

He walked into the kitchen of his apartment, perked some coffee and tried to sober up a bit. He surely didn't need a DUI right now. He might say something that would tie him to Tom's problems.

A couple of hours later, he drove toward Los Lunas to the old farmhouse where he had grown up. It was all boarded up now, and had been since his parents passed away. The fencerows were grown up in sunflowers and Johnson grass that would have upset his father very much. His father had always kept them weed-free when he was alive. The old cottonwood trees had already been through the process of turning gold and most of the leaves were in piles all along the dirt road. They flew into the air and crunched under the vehicle tires as he slowly drove down the unpaved lane, trying to avoid the deep ruts which had washed out from the rain over the years.

His parents had made a provision in their will that after he inherited the farm, he could not sell it until after twenty years of their passing or else seventy-five per cent of the proceeds would go to the First Baptist Church. Grant wasn't about to give up that kind of money to a church, and the land was just increasing in value every year. He could wait. It would only be another seven years. Then he would be wealthy. Just seven more years.

The electricity had been shut off for years so there would be no lights to turn on in the house. He took a flashlight out of his vehicle and went into the old farm house. Everything was covered in thick dust, with spider webs hanging from the light fixtures and across the door openings. He had covered the furniture with sheets when he boarded up the windows, but other than that, it looked pretty much like it had when his parents were alive. Grant marveled that vandals or illegal aliens hadn't broken in and used the property, but it was still intact.

Grant opened the door from the kitchen to the stairs that led down into the basement. He swung the flashlight beam around through the darkness, shining the spray of light over the shelves where his mother stored her jars of canned fruits and vegetables. There were no windows. The basement had one large room then a short hallway leading into a bedroom and beyond that a small bathroom. It was pitch black without the flashlight.

This will be perfect. He wandered through the musty-smelling darkness and stifled the emotions welling up in his mind as memories of his family flitted through his mind. His mother would be devastated if she knew of his beer drinking and use of cocaine. However, his parents would never know how he had changed. He shook off the bad feelings of nostalgia.

After checking out the old farmhouse, Grant headed back to his apartment. Now he would be able to use one of the items he had lifted from Pamela Johnson's veterinary medicine cabinet.

*

Ginger was still thinking about the meeting with Ava Grissom when she pulled up to the mailbox out in front of the Howell Estate. *That Alfred Benedetti gives me the creeps.* She stopped within a few feet of the community mailbox and got out her key. She left the car door open as she walked over to the box and leaned over to unlock it.

Grant had been waiting for her. When he saw her car turn into the lane, he quietly got out of his car which was parked behind a stand of trees, and walked up to a vantage point out of Ginger's sight.

As Ginger leaned over, Grant walked silently up behind her. Using his left arm to circle around her body and hold her tight, he brought his right hand up to cover her nose and mouth with a handkerchief he had saturated with chloroform.

Ginger struggled for a moment before she took a breath of the chloroform, and then sank to the ground, unconscious. Grant held the hanky in place for another couple of minutes, to make sure she wouldn't wake up immediately, then picked her up, carried her to his car and drove away.

***

Chapter Twenty-Six

Tom Howell was home early for a change and he thought he would surprise Ginger by grilling a couple of steaks for dinner. It was Maggie's night off, Bertha and Trey had eaten early and retired to their suite, and the Howell estate had settled into the pastoral quietness of the typical North Valley evening.

Everything was just about ready. He had peeled potatoes and sliced them into quarter-inch thick coins and arranged them in layers in aluminum foil he had coated with cooking oil, sprinkled them with salt and pepper, and sealed up the foil packets. He would put these on the grill with the steaks. He had picked up a prepared package of Romaine lettuce to make Caesar salad, and the marinated rib-eye steaks were ready to throw on the grill.

"Where the heck are you, Ginger?" he said aloud, looking at his watch.

Scooter, the little Yorkie, looked up at him, cocked his head to one side, then turned to look at the back door, as if expecting Ginger to walk through it any minute.

"She's late, isn't she, little buddy," he said to the dog.

Tom turned on the television, to catch the evening news until Ginger got home. Fifteen minutes later, he was still drumming his fingers on the chair arm, and beginning to get irritated. He picked up his cell phone and dialed the store, thinking she might have last minute things to do there. No answer. Everyone had already gone home. Next, he dialed Ginger's cell phone. It rang four or five times before her voice came on the phone asking the caller to leave a message.

"Where do you think she is, Scooter? If she doesn't show up pretty soon, I'm going to cook these steaks anyway, and hers will just be cold."

After thirty minutes had passed, Tom tried Ginger's cell phone for the third time, and again got the voice mail option.

"This just isn't like her—to be so late and not call. Maybe she had car trouble between here and the store, and forgot to turn on her cell phone. What do you think, Scooter-boy? Should I take a run to the store and see if she's somewhere in between?"

Tom put the steak, potatoes, and salad back into the refrigerator and walked purposefully out to his car. When he got down the lane, he immediately saw Ginger's car, still running and with the door open, parked at the mailbox. Ginger was nowhere to be seen.

Tom pulled up beside the car and quickly took in the scene. Ginger's purse was still on the seat of her car. Her key to the mailbox was on the ground by the support post. Panic rose in Tom's throat. He called out to her.

"Ginger, if you are around here someplace, this is *not funny!*" Silence.

Since Pete Lucero's number was loaded into his cell phone, Tom quickly dialed it.

"Pete, this is Tom Howell. I don't think this is the right department for this phone call, but with all that's happened, I'm in a panic, and I had your number handy." He quickly described the scene to Pete. "It just isn't like her to be late and not call—then her car looks like she just disappeared into thin air while she was trying to open the mailbox. I don't know what to do next."

"Try to be calm, Tom. I am off work, and I haven't got a thing to do right now. I'll call a couple of black and whites that are in the neighborhood. Don't walk around or touch anything—I'll be there in fifteen minutes." said Pete quickly.

Pete made it to the scene in twelve minutes. "It was just like this when you found her car, Tom?" he asked.

"Except for the fact that I turned off the ignition. The car was still running when I got here. I came to look for her when she didn't show up after forty-five minutes, and wasn't answering her cell phone. Now I know why she didn't answer. Her cell phone is in her purse on the seat of the car." Tom ran his fingers through his dark blond hair.

"With all that has happened the past few weeks, Tom, I'm going to treat this like a kidnapping. It's not my department, thank God, as it isn't a homicide, but I can work with them on this. Right now it's getting pretty dark, but I'll have these patrolmen carefully look for footprints around the perimeter, and see if anything turns up."

Five minutes later, one of the patrolmen came up to Pete and said, "Looks like a car was parked behind that stand of trees over there. There are two sets of footprints in the dirt. One coming this way and the other going back to the car. There are no female prints, but the set going back to the car are much deeper than the ones coming this way."

"Might mean he was carrying someone?"

"That's what I was thinking," responded the patrolman.

That conversation was out of Tom's hearing. He was talking on his cell phone to his son, Jon, to let him know what was happening.

"Is there anything we can do, Dad?" asked Jon.

"Pray. That's about the only option open to us right now, son. Just pray."

"Let us know immediately if you find her, Dad," said Jon. "We'll do whatever we can to help."

"God, I don't know what to do! I think it's just a waiting game right now, son. If she has been kidnapped, then we will probably be hearing from the guy about a ransom. We'll pay whatever is necessary to get your Mom back, I promise you."

"Maybe we ought to come on down to be with you."

"Hold on a minute, Jon. Pete Lucero might have some information."

Pete walked over to Tom and put a hand on his shoulder. "I'm going to come home with you, Tom, just in case someone calls you about this. Maybe she will come home on her own, but it looks pretty suspicious, to me." Pete then told Tom about the car tire tracks and the footprints.

"Okay. I'll be glad to have your company. I'm going to feel foolish if she just decided to catch a ride to the grocery store with a neighbor and just spaced out turning off the ignition and shutting the car door—although that isn't like her." Tom turned to finish his call to his son, "Lucero will stay down here until we hear something, Son. There's no point in having you pace the floor with me. I'll be sure to call you as soon as we get any information at all."

***

Chapter Twenty-Seven

Ginger slowly opened her eyes, blinking, groggy from the drug, and was startled that she couldn't see anything. *I can't open my eyes, or else I have gone blind!* She was lying down on a hard surface and was stiff from being cold. She rubbed her arms briskly to get some feeling back into them.

It was totally dark. There was not even a pinpoint of light in the small room in which she lay. She raised her hand toward her face, but could not make out the shape of her hand. Gradually coming out of the drug stupor, she began to panic. *Where am I? What has happened to me?*

She shook her head, trying to remember. She had stopped at the mailbox, still thinking about Ava Grissom and Alfred Benedetti, she remembered. *But why can't I see?*

She cautiously turned on one elbow and raised her head slightly. With the other hand, she reached out slowly, groping for anything that might be in front of her. She knew that she had her eyes open, but there was only total darkness.

Panic rose in her mind, and she tried her voice. "HELP!" she croaked. "Somebody please help me!" She listened for a response, but the silence was as thick as the darkness. Not a sound. Nothing. Blackness.

Where am I? she wondered. *Could I be dead? Is this what death is like?* She was terrified.

Minutes passed as Ginger tried to calm the panic. She gingerly felt all the way around herself. The floor was cold and hard, with a thick layer of dust on it, but it was smooth. Like linoleum, or wood planks. Her fingers explored the surface of the floor. There were grout lines. The floor had ceramic tile on it.

Her fingers next bumped into a hard object. It was cold and smooth. She felt along the surface as far as she could reach, and then started up from the floor. About eighteen inches up, the surface turned away from her for about four inches, then down. *This is a bathtub!* She recognized the shape. Getting to her knees, she bumped her head hard into the bottom of a pedestal lavatory.

"Ow!" Ginger briefly saw stars inside her head from the hard knock on top of her head. "That hurt!" she said aloud, rubbing the bump. Carefully she groped around behind her and felt the commode. "At least I now know that I am in a bathroom, I wonder if there is some water? Maybe I could splash some on my face and wake up. If my head didn't hurt so much, I'd think this is probably just a nightmare."

She yelled again as loudly as she could, "HELP! Is anyone there?" Silence.

Gradually she felt her way around the room trying to locate the light switch. She flipped it up and down several times with no results. No lights came on. She then felt for the other fixtures to get her bearings. Cautiously getting to her feet she stretched her hands as high as she could reach. She could not reach anything above her head. She then groped for the bowl of the lavatory and located the faucets.

Please let there be some water! she thought. She turned the right hand tap slowly. It gurgled and spit, but finally a trickle of water came through the spigot. She let it run for a few moments, and carefully touched her tongue to the water that she caught in her hand. It seemed to be a bit stale, but drinkable. She splashed a couple of handfuls of water on her face. She decided to try calling out once more. "Hello! Is anybody there? Hello! Please come and help me!" No answer. Complete silence. Total darkness. Chilled air. The temperature in the room was probably about sixty-four degrees. It was bearable, but certainly not in Ginger's comfort level. She rubbed her arms vigorously, trying to get warm.

She spent the next few minutes feeling her way completely around the small room. It might have been six feet wide, and seven feet long. She discovered the door and tried the knob. Locked! She jerked on the knob several times, but it was very solid and secure. She kicked the bottom of the door, but only succeeded in hurting her toes.

She continued to feel around the room. There were some shelves above the commode, which held a couple of towels, several washcloths, and a cylindrical box of powdered cleanser. On the back of the lavatory there was a dried out bar of soap, a toothbrush holder with two toothbrushes in it, a pump action dispenser that might have held hand lotion, and an empty glass.

She filled the glass about half full of water and drank it. *At least I won't die of thirst!* Reaching behind her, she put the lid down on the commode and sat down on it. *Hmm. I wonder if it works?.* She reached behind and pulled down the lever. It made a coughing sound, because the water in the tank had apparently evaporated away. The water gushed into the tank, and noisily filled it to the proper water line. *I guess I have toilet facilities, too!*

She sat there on the closed lid of the commode, wondering what to do next. She felt like her eyes were open as far as they could possibly open, seeking light. Total darkness. She waved her hands around in front of her face. She couldn't see them.

Who would do this to me? she thought. "I'll bet that it's the same nut that has been giving Tom such a hassle. But for what purpose? To bug Tom, of course!" she said, suddenly understanding. "Tom must be going crazy wondering what has happened to me. That nut is trying to give Tom a nervous breakdown." The idea made her really angry. "Hey, you pervert! You come here and let me out! Do you hear me?" she screamed. "Let me out of here!" She felt her way to the door and banged on it with her fists. No answer. "Not here, huh?

Well you will be back, and when you get back, I'll be waiting for you, you jerk!" Sudden tears welled up in her eyes and rolled unbidden down her cheeks. "Oh, no. I'm not going to cry!" She choked back the sobs and wiped the tears off her face with the back of her hand. She had no concept of what time it was, not knowing how long she had been unconscious. Her watch had a quartz crystal, so there was not even the sound of a ticking watch.

The anger returned, but she controlled it by trying to think of how she might have gotten into this fix. *I remember stopping to get the mail, then this arm grabbed me from behind and he stuck something over my nose and mouth. I couldn't breathe. I must have passed out. Whoever it was drugged me. It must have been chloroform! Who was it?* A vision of Alfred Benedetti appeared in her mind, but that just didn't seem logical. What purpose could he possibly have? *Ransom? That's ridiculous. He wouldn't know about my mailbox. He must have been waiting for me...or did he follow me home?*

Time seemed to drag by, even though Ginger had no reference to tell how much time had passed since she awoke on the floor of the bathroom. A sudden sound startled her. *What was that? A growl?* The sound repeated itself, and Ginger felt foolish. It was her stomach. She hadn't eaten anything since lunchtime, and she was hungry. Thinking that maybe water would fill her up for the moment, Ginger filled the glass and drank two full glasses of water. The growling stopped, at least temporarily. *Thank goodness the toilet works,* she thought. Suddenly she remembered that she had stuck a package of cheddar cheese and peanut butter crackers in the pocket of her sweater. She carefully counted out the number of crackers in the package. *Six. If I just knew how long I'd be here, I could ration the crackers.* "That's silly. I have no idea how long it will take for Tom to find me. I'll try to space them out as long as I can hold out, without starving. Besides, I might even lose a few pounds." Talking aloud to herself seemed to have a calming effect. "I wonder where I am? There is no sound at all, so it must not be in the city. It's got to be out in the country and from the dust and the shape of these fixtures, this house may have been abandoned for years."

"Okay," she continued, as she nibbled on one of the crackers, "Let me go over everything that has happened. I should be able to figure out who would do this to Tom and me." There was a soft rug in front of the bathtub. "Guess I might as well get comfortable. No telling how long this idiot is going to keep me here." She took some of the towels from the shelf to make a pillow, and lay down on the rug in front of the tub. She then started thinking back over everything that had happened since the first incident….the magazines and credit cards that started coming in by the bushel basket load, the ipecac, Nicki's murder, the computer crash, the flat tires, the cut brake line, Syd's accident, the store burning down….and now this….

***

Chapter Twenty-Eight

Tom and Pete Lucero spent most of the night sitting by the telephone, hoping that it would ring. It didn't.

"This just has to be tied to the Nicolette du Pree murder, doesn't it?" asked Tom.

"Not necessarily," replied Pete. "However, you never know what some nut is going to dream up in this world. There is a connection however remote between you and Nicki, but Ginger's disappearance may not have anything to do with her. I don't see any connection at all between the murder and having the brake line cut on your vehicle, or having your tires slashed, unless they were trying to kill you. That seems more of a vandalism or revenge thing than anything else. Have you fired anyone lately from the store?"

"No, and not for the past two or three years. And all of the staff seems to be pretty happy with their jobs right now, as far as I can tell."

"We have sort of eliminated Mike Stevens as a suspect in the murder case. He was so crazy about Nicki, that I can't see him wanting her dead. Now if it had been Dr. Coco..uh, Ciccone that wound up dead, He would be a suspect in that murder."

"Mike was pretty broken-hearted when Nicki moved him out and Dr. Ciccone moved in."

"Ciccone puts up a pretty macho image, but I wonder if Nicki got to him a bit more than he let on?"

"That's possible. He's not getting any younger, and it might be that he's tiring of the chase. He was pretty smitten by Nicki. You don't think that he killed her, do you?"

"We thought at first that he might have a good motive, but he had an alibi for the time of death. He said he was dancing, but couldn't remember the names of the women. Paula agreed that he was on the dance floor, gave us the lady's name, and she confirmed the time. *He* didn't kill Nicki. Does the dear doctor have any problems with you?"

"I barely know the guy. We've played a few rounds of golf in the same foursome and he is a member of the Club, but other than that, I don't know anything about him."

"What about Bud Simpson? Are you on his black list for something?"

"I don't think so. I don't know him any better than I know Ciccone. Bud has no love for Grant McGuire, though."

"Speaking of McGuire, have you seen him lately?"

"Matter of fact, I talked to him for a few minutes just before you joined us for lunch at the club. He was telling me how sorry he was about the fire," said Tom.

"Did he have anything else to say?"

"He said he was surprised I hadn't had a nervous breakdown yet. I told him that I probably would never have made it except for Ginger."

Pete pursed his lips, scratched the back of his neck, and said, "You made it pretty clear that you would never make it without Ginger, and now Ginger is missing…strange, isn't it?"

"You don't think that Grant…? Why, we've been friends for years. He was my college roommate!"

"But you have been very successful. He told us that Nicki wanted financial security and his finances were in such a mess that he couldn't give it to her. What's his personal situation?"

"Well, not good. He's been divorced four times. He has four children with three different mothers. Lots of child support. Sadly, one of the children is mentally challenged."

"And you have been married to this great little lady for how long?"

"Over forty years."

"And your children?"

"I have two. Both of them are financially independent, married, and doing well."

"Could it be that he can't stand your success, and that he has been trying to make it as tough on you as life has been on him?"

"Well, he can't beat me playing golf," laughed Tom, "but surely he wouldn't resort to taking Ginger by force." he finished the sentence on a serious note.

"Well, he admitted to using cocaine, and doesn't he drink quite a bit as well?"

"I've noticed that it has been getting progressively worse, lately. Seems like he always has a can of beer in his hand."

"If we don't hear tonight from Ginger, or whoever took her, then I suggest that the both of us have a talk with Grant McGuire in the morning." said Pete.

The worry was causing Tom's stomach to burn. He popped an antacid into his mouth and ran his fingers through his hair. He looked at the telephone, wishing it would ring.

*

Meanwhile, Ginger had given herself a headache trying to concentrate on all of the bad things that had happened to Tom. She finally fell into a fitful sort of sleep lying there on the floor by the bathtub. When she woke, she bumped her elbow on the tub. Both of her legs were tingling from lack of circulation. She lay in one position too long as she slept with her knees bent toward the ceiling and didn't have room to stretch out her legs. She shivered with cold. At first, she didn't remember where she was and had forgotten about it being completely dark in the room.

She decided to try screaming again. "HELP! Somebody please help me! Anybody there?" No answer. Complete silence. Total darkness.

"I can't believe this is happening to me." she fumed. There was a bad taste in her mouth and she ached from lying on the cold, hard floor. As she started to stand up, she felt something fabric. Holding onto it she tried to pull herself up.

CRASH!

"What on earth," she yelled. Feeling her way, she discovered that she had gotten hold of the shower curtain. When she pulled on it, the tension bar holding it up came loose and crashed into the tub. Feeling her way, she unthreaded the curtain holders from the pole, unsnapped the hooks that held the curtain, and now at least had a piece of fabric that she could use for a blanket. She folded the shower curtain's plastic liner, and felt her way to the shelf above the commode and stored it out of the way.

"I wonder if the hot water heater is working?" she asked aloud. "Let's find out." She felt rather foolish, talking to herself, but it kept her spirits a little higher to hear something, even if it was her own voice. She turned on the hot water tap and let it run for several minutes. Still cold. They had probably turned off the gas service as well as the electricity.

"Well, that eliminates the thought of a hot bath! However, maybe it would be more comfortable sitting in the bathtub than on the commode or on the floor. At least I could lean back a little bit." She took the rug and shook it just a little. Dust flew everywhere, and Ginger started coughing from breathing it in.

"Whew! Bad idea. Don't shake the rug!" She felt to see which side was the right side, then spread the rug on the bottom of the tub, rolled up the towels she was using for a pillow, climbed into the tub and tried to cover herself with the shower curtain for warmth. The darkness settled around her, punctuated by the complete silence.

"Yea, though I walk through the valley of the shadow of death, I shall fear no evil, for Thou art with me. Thy rod and Thy staff, they comfort me." Quoting the Twenty-Third Psalm seemed to give her courage. "I wonder if I can remember all of it," she said aloud, then started at the beginning. "The Lord is my Shepherd...."

*

The next morning, Tom and Pete were served a large breakfast by Maggie and Bertha. Tom was too worried to eat, and didn't have the courage to tell Maggie that Ginger was missing. There had been no phone call, no ransom demand. There was no word of Ginger, period.

After breakfast, Pete assured Tom that he would get in touch with the proper authorities and put out a missing person's bulletin for his wife as soon as the law allowed.

"I just had a thought. Pete, can we keep Ginger's disappearance from the media until I have a chance to talk to Grant McGuire? If he knows that Ginger is missing, and it hasn't come out yet, then it would probably mean that he had something to do with her disappearance. What do you think?"

"That's not a bad idea. Since there was no ransom demand, the police won't even consider it a missing person right away, even under the circumstances. We wouldn't want to wait long, however, as the first hours after someone goes missing are the most critical. I'll have to call the Police Captain with APD and have him put a gag order on the report from the officers that responded to my call last night. Hopefully none of our illustrious media people were listening to their police scanners last night, and even if they were there probably has not been enough time to make the papers or news broadcasts yet."

*

Tom drove over to Grant's apartment and rang the bell. Pete drove his own vehicle, and waited in the car until Tom was in the apartment.

"Tom! What are you doing here? You look terrible." Grant was startled by Tom's appearance.

"Oh, I didn't get much sleep last night. May I come in?"

"Sorry, come right on in. Would you like a cup of coffee?"

"Maybe about a gallon—black—as you know," replied Tom.

"I'm really surprised to see you this morning," said Grant, as he poured the coffee, then set the pot down.

"Why is that, Grant?"

"I just thought that you would have more important things to do this morning, with Ginger missing, and all."

"And how did you know that Ginger was missing?" asked Tom, innocently.

"Why, the radio, it's all over town by now, isn't it?"

"You dirty slime ball! What have you done with my wife?" Tom stood up and started after Grant.

Grant backed up, and kept going backwards as Tom advanced. "What are you saying, Tom?" he cried.

"The media has not heard about Ginger's disappearance. You had something to do with it, or you wouldn't have known it. And how about all this other crap that's been going on? Is that all your doing, too?" By now Tom had Grant backed up against the sink in the kitchen, with a handful of his shirt in his left hand. His right hand was cocked and ready to fly, right into Grant's face. Pete had been waiting just outside the front door, and hearing the yelling, hurried on into the room.

"Don't hit me! Don't hit me!" cried Grant. He was a coward from the word go, and couldn't stand the thought of getting hurt.

"Where is Ginger?" yelled Tom. "What have you done with my wife?" When Grant didn't answer, Tom hit him in the face with his fist. Blood spurted from Grant's nose and ran down his chin. "Tell me what you have done with Ginger!" Tom yelled.

Grant put his hands over his face, and when he saw Pete, squeaked, "Don't let him hit me again! Please!" he begged.

"Back off, Tom, I think that Mr. McGuire might like to come downtown and talk to the police rather than to face you. Is that right, Mr. McGuire?"

"He always wins, he always gets the best, he always gets the right girl, has the successful kids, gets elected President of the club! Mr. Have-It-All! Just like my big brother! I could never do anything right. Still can't. My father was right." Grant completely dissolved into a puddle on the kitchen floor, screaming and crying. Sobs shook his entire body.

"Come on Mr. McGuire, we're going downtown. You have a lot of questions to answer." Pete took Grant's arm and propelled him out the door to his unmarked police car. If you follow us downtown, Tom, we might find out what he has done with Ginger."

***

Chapter Twenty-Nine

Dr. Antonio Ciccone decided to check on the progress that Ricky the Rat was making on the project he had given him. He dialed the number from memory.

"H'lo," was the muffled reply.

"Is it okay to talk?" asked Ciccone.

"Yeah, I've got a minute."

"Are you any closer to that thousand dollars?"

"Do you have the money now?" asked Ricky.

"Right here in my hand. I can have it to the bartender in a half-hour."

"He'll have th' name when you get there with the dough," said Ricky. Click. He hung up.

This might be worth the thousand, just to see whose name comes up, thought Ciccone.

He was at the Silver Eagle Bar in twenty minutes. He handed an envelope to the bartender, who looked briefly through the cash.

"Ricky said you would give him money for this envelope," said the bartender, handing it to Dr. Ciccone.

Ciccone opened the sealed envelope, looked at the name and left the bar. He went straight to the office of Homicide Investigations and asked for Pete Lucero.

"Homicide Detective Lucero is out at the moment. Would you like to speak to his partner, Homicide Detective Patrick

Mahoney?" She moved her chewing gum to the other side of her mouth, pushed her thick glasses back up on her nose, patted her mousy brown hair, and shifted her voluminous bottom that overhung the secretarial chair on both sides.

"Yes, please," responded Dr. Ciccone. He still couldn't believe that voice, the voice of an angel, came out of that body.

"Mahoney says to go right on back. Do you know which office is his?" asked the voice.

"Yes, thank you." Ciccone hurried down the hall to Patrick's office.

"Good morning, Dr. Ciccone," said Pat pleasantly. "What may I do for you this morning?"

"I have some information for you. You will have to be the one to decide how important it is."

"Okay. What is it?"

"I would rather not say how or where I obtained this information," said the doctor, "but this name was given to me by someone who should know this sort of thing. He claims that this man obtained sodium pentobarbital, without a prescription. It could be tied to Nicki's death." He handed the envelope to Patrick.

"Big Al? And who is Big Al?"

"I'm not sure, but I think his full name is Alfred Benedetti. He is rumored to have connections to organized crime."

"We will certainly look into this, Dr. Ciccone. We weren't able to bring this item up on our computers."

"I would think not."

"Of course we will have to verify the information, but I would like to thank you for bringing this information to our attention."

"Certainly. At any rate, you're welcome, and maybe it will bring you closer to Nicki's killer. It's about time that I should admit that I was really in love with the girl. I would have married her in a heartbeat, but she rejected the idea."

As the doctor left the building, Pete Lucero brought Grant McGuire into the building through a side entrance.

Pete took Grant into an interrogation office and settled him into a chair.

"I suggest that you try to settle down, get control of your emotions, and get ready to answer some tough questions, Mr. McGuire."

Tom was ushered into an observation room, where he could watch the interrogation through a one-way glass window. He would be able to see and hear everything, without Grant's knowledge.

Pete went back to his office for some files and stuck his head into Patrick's office. "Well, I got my wish."

"How's that, Pete?" asked Patrick.

"Looks like I'm going to get to file some charges against that asshole, Grant McGuire. He's in Interrogation Room Two. Wanna join me?"

Patrick's eyebrows flew up. "No kidding! You bet I want to join you."

The two homicide detectives went in together to question Grant.

"We will be taping this conversation, Mr. McGuire. Read him his rights, Patrick," said Pete.

Patrick complied with the request.

"Feel free to tell your story from the beginning," said Pete as he pushed the *record* button.

Grant spent the next two hours telling the detectives how his father had always praised his older brother, and how he was always the klutz. He then proceeded to explain his relationship with Tom Howell—how they were such good friends in college, shared so many experiences, but how gradually over the years Tom had ended up taking the place of his older brother, who always did everything right, while his own life was falling apart.

Grant admitted to the magazine subscriptions, the store credit cards, the ipecac, the slashed tires, the cut brake line, the arson of the store, and kidnapping Ginger Howell.

"Every time that I would come up with something I thought would bring him down, he just kept coming right back. He was like one of those little balls that the harder you bounce it the higher it keeps going. I really didn't intend for the granddaughter to get hurt. I knew that Tom would be able to handle it, but it would be another nuisance. I didn't count on him lending his car to Sydney. Then, I thought for sure the fire would take him down a notch. He and Ginger still seemed to bounce right back. But when he said he didn't think he could make it without her, then I knew she had to go."

Tom caught his breath, waiting for what Grant would say next—praying that he had not hurt her—or worse.

"So exactly where is Ginger Howell?" asked Patrick.

"She is alive." He looked up and smiled—a devious glint in his eyes, "This might be the last chance I have to get back at Tom Howell for all his successes. I'm not going to tell you where she is."

Tom bounded up from his chair. They could not hear him through the glass, and it was probably a good thing he couldn't be heard.

"So what are the charges against me?" asked Grant.

"What about Nicolette du Pree?" asked Pete.

"Nicki? I didn't have anything to do with that."

"By your own admission, we know that you were lovers. You used cocaine together. You were in the building the night of the murder. You had access to the sodium pentobarbital that killed Nicki when you went to Pamela Johnson's home. The circumstantial evidence is mounting. You go ahead and confess; maybe the D.A. will cut you a deal. Life, instead of the death penalty." said Pete.

Grant suddenly wasn't so cocky any more. "But I promise you, I didn't have anything to do with killing Nicki!"

"Where is Ginger Howell?"

"I'd rather not say."

"If something happens that Ginger isn't returned safe and sound, I'd hate to be in your shoes, buddy," stated Pete.

Patrick called a jailer to take Grant into custody.

"I want to call my lawyer!" cried Grant.

"Fine. Let him call his lawyer—and then throw him in the lock-up," Pete said to the jailer.

"What are the charges? I'll need to tell my attorney."

"You seemed to have a pretty good knowledge of your "rights". Start with suspicion of the first degree murder of Nicolette du Pree, kidnapping, arson, malicious vandalism, attempted murder, and we'll see if we can think of a few more!" yelled Pete as he walked purposefully out of the room, leaving McGuire protesting his innocence of killing Nicki.

Tom was waiting for Pete when he came out of the interrogation room.

"Why can't we make him tell us where he has Ginger?" Tom demanded.

"I'm sorry, Tom. Short of torturing him or forcing him to be injected with truth serum, I don't know what else we can do. The District Attorney will have to come up with the formal charges, but short of some kind of "deal", Grant may have us over a barrel."

"Let me have him for just five minutes. He'll tell me where she is!" cried Tom, doubling up his fists. Pete looked up quickly.

"I am sure of that, and I don't blame you a bit. Maybe Patrick can dream up some way of forcing the information out of him. He's good at stuff like that."

"With a taped confession, I don't know how he could possibly think he had any power to make any kind of deal."

"Lawyers can always claim that the confession was under coercion, and he could retract his confession. Especially if they take pictures of that swollen jaw, nose, and black eye you laid on him. They'll probably come back with some charge of assault against *you*."

***

Chapter Thirty

After Grant McGuire was arrested Tom called his daughter to let her know that Ginger was missing. Leslie was devastated with the news and made airline reservations immediately to return to Albuquerque from her home in Hawaii.

"Dad, I *have* to come! I know that I probably won't be able to help find Mom, but I need to be with you and the rest of the family."

"I understand, Les. We'll pick you up at the airport when you get here."

"Isn't there *something* that I could do to help find her?"

"We are at our wit's end, Leslie. Jon and his family are here with me, and we've been wracking our brains for any kind of clue. I'm kicking myself all over the place for not recognizing what a louse Grant is, even after your Mom warned me about him. It's all my fault that she's missing. I'm about to go crazy with worry."

"It can't be your fault, Dad. Hang in there. Surely the police will come up with something soon, or make that nut tell us what he has done with Mom."

"We can only hope so, Babe. We'll see you in a few hours."

Five days later Grant had still not revealed where he had stashed Ginger, and he continued to deny having anything to do with Nicki's murder. Tom was a nervous wreck. He had broken out in hives and had not slept more than a few minutes at a time since Ginger disappeared.

    Jon, Judith, Brandon, Sydney, and "J" had spent most of the five days at the Howell Estate, along with Leslie, trying to figure out how to go about finding Ginger.

"Dad, you've simply got to take care of yourself, or you're not going to be in any condition to help find Mom, at all." said Jon.

Tom took another big gulp of hot coffee that Maggie had poured him, and ran his fingers through his hair. "I can't believe I was so stupid. I should have seen right through Grant's act. Your Mother tried to tell me he wasn't shooting straight, and I ignored her. If we don't find her soon, I ..." his voice trailed off.

Judith looked up suddenly. "I just had an idea," she said. "Let's put ourselves into Grant's shoes. Didn't you tell us a story one time about going to visit his parents somewhere close to Albuquerque?"

Tom sat up straighter in his chair, struggling to remember. "I… think….so. Yes. Grant took me out to this farm where his parents lived. We went quail hunting. Hunting was about all we did, though. I don't think we saw a single bird."

"Do you know if his parents are still alive?" asked Jon.

"I'm sure they are both gone. Seems like they passed away within a few weeks of each other several years ago. I went to both funerals," said Tom. "I remember trying to console Grant. He was pretty broken up. I am so exhausted that it is difficult to remember anything."

"You have mentioned how Grant went through bankruptcy two or three times, so he probably doesn't have any property of his own, but do you think his parent's place would still be in the family name?"

"Why don't you call Lucero or Mahoney? They can probably find out using their computer. If I wasn't so tired, I might even be able to pull up the property tax rolls on my own computer," said Tom. "I keep having these nightmares about what your mother might be going through."

Patrick took the call from Jon Howell. "How is your Dad holding up, Jon?" he asked.

"Not very well, as you can imagine. I'm not either, for that matter. However, my wife, Judith, came up with an idea, and we need your help," he replied.

"Happy to help any way I can. What is it you need?"

"She thought perhaps Grant would have taken my Mom out to his folk's old home place in the country. Is there any way you can find out if there is some property still owned by the McGuire family?"

"That's easy enough. Do you know the parent's first names?"

"Dad didn't remember, but he thought that they had both passed away ten to fifteen years ago."

"That would be a matter of public record. I can certainly pull that up on Dora in a matter of a few minutes. Do you want to wait, or shall I call you back?"

"Better call me back." He gave Patrick the number.

Dora hummed and buzzed as Patrick's fingers flew over the keyboard.

"Whatcha up to?" asked Pete, sticking his head in the door.

"The Howell case."

*

Ginger had settled into a routine of doing isometric exercises, quoting scripture, stretching, and singing every song that she could remember, even if she had to make up some of the words. She slept in the bathtub. The silence was almost as bad as the darkness and she began to imagine that she could hear someone speak to her. She was extremely cold and hungry. By now, she had eaten the six cheddar cheese and peanut butter crackers that were in her pocket.

She had no concept of time. Without light there was no night or day; no sunset or sunrise; no clock to tell her how many minutes, hours, or days she had been held captive. The cold had chilled her to the bone, and the darkness surrounding her tested her endurance to the limit. At one point, an incident occurred that almost put her into hysterics.

She was working on isometric exercises— stretched out between the lavatory and the commode with her feet touching the side of the bathtub. She thought she felt something moving on her arm. She casually reached down to scratch the sensation, and jumped straight up from the floor to her feet! It was a cockroach!

"Yiiiii!" she yelled. "Get off of me! Get off of me!" She started stomping her feet to try to shake the insect off of her body. She shuddered with revulsion! "I HATE COCKROACHES!" she screamed at the top of her lungs and then broke into uncontrollable sobbing.

Fully awake now, she shook the rug on which she had been sleeping. The air was already stale, as the only fresh oxygen that came into the dark room was filtered through the plumbing vents, and those vents did not lead directly to the outside. The dust that filled the room when she shook the rug filled her lungs and she went into a fit of coughing.

She turned on the water and cupped it into her mouth with her hand, trying to clear the dust. She then pulled her blouse up over her nose, to try to keep from breathing the fine dust. After a while, she managed to stop coughing, the dust settled, and her heart rate dropped back into an almost normal range.

Her emotions fluctuated between anger, hope, helplessness, frustration, and despair. The only things that kept her from losing complete control were the thoughts of her family, the scriptures that she could remember, and the prayers that were always on her lips. Not knowing the hours or days she had spent in the totally black room, there was one thought in the back of her mind—she knew Tom was looking for her, and he would find her.

Philippians 4:13 popped into her mind—*I can do all things through Christ who strengthens me.*

When this thought came into her mind, Ginger was a changed woman. The only way out of the room was through the locked door. She didn't have any way to unlock it—not even a bobby pin to try to pick the lock. She might be able to cut through the door panel with some of the plumbing, if she could get any of it loose. *I can't afford to dismantle the toilet, but maybe I can get something loose from the drain in the sink!* With that thought in mind, she felt for the lavatory, and began trying to pull out the drain stopper. *If I can get something to use to push with, I might be able to tap the bolts out of the hinges on the door!*

With a plan in mind, Ginger doubled her efforts of dismantling the drain. *There is a knob behind the faucet that closes the drain when I pull it up! Maybe I can unscrew it or something.*

Her hand slipped, causing her knuckles to hit the wall behind the faucet, breaking the skin. "Ouch!" she cried, immediately putting the skinned knuckles into her mouth to try to stop the flow of blood. "That's okay," she said aloud. "I just don't want to get it infected." She waited until she was sure the bleeding has stopped before she once again tackled the drain. Working totally in the dark, it was hard to determine exactly what kind of progress she was making.

"Finally!" she cried, as the part came free. "Now let me see if I can find the bottom of the hinge…and I'm going to need to hit it with something." She felt her way over to the door and carefully felt for the bottom of the hinge. My shoe! "I can hit this sucker with the heel of my shoe." she decided.

Remembering the cockroach, she removed her shoe, and carefully put that foot down on the floor, then turned to the task at hand. With the first tap, she dropped the thin rod and it clattered to the floor.

"Oh no you don't!" she said. "It took me too long to get you out of that sink. You're not going anywhere." Her hands were clumsy and stiff with cold. She knelt down, and started feeling around on the floor for the thin metal rod. It had rolled over against the baseboard and she spent several minutes feeling along the floor until she finally located it. "Easy does it. I've got to make another effort to try to push out the hinge bolt. I've got to be careful now, but it's going to take some force with my shoe to make this thing move." It gave her some confidence simply to hear her own voice in the silence.

After the tenth hit with the shoe heel, Ginger finally felt a little movement. The bolt had slipped up inside the hinge a quarter-inch. "Aha! You can move," said cried triumphantly. She was breathing hard and shaking with the effort of trying to dislodge the bolt. "All right. I'm going to take a little breather now, but I'll be back." It was encouraging for her to even have a plan. It might take a long time, but it was something to do. She slowly drank a full glass of water, and arranged the rug back into the tub. Rolling herself up in the shower curtain and crawling into the tub, she quickly fell asleep from exhaustion.

***

Chapter Thirty-One

Alfred Benedetti knew he was in trouble. He had not been able to find Nicki's nanny. She and the little redheaded kid seemed to have vanished into thin air. Not only that, this Ava Grissom was a royal pain in the neck. If the Big Man had not made it a direct order, he would have ditched this old broad a long time ago.

"Hey Al, would you bring me another cup of coffee, please" requested Ava.

"Get it yourself, you old bag," he muttered quietly under his breath.

"What did you say?" asked Ava, from the other room.

"I said, I'll be happy to," said Al, raising his voice. He lumbered over to the coffee pot.

"When is the Man supposed to be back in town, Al?" Ava asked when he brought in the coffee.

"He was going to be gone for three weeks, he said, so I think that means he will be back tomorrow," replied Al.

"Hmm. I think he'll be pleased with the progress we've made so far. Some joker bought us some time when he kidnapped our landlord. Pretty lucky, don't you think?"

"Yeah, lucky." said Al flatly.

"You think he killed her?" asked Ava. Al shrugged.

"In any case, we should have everything running pretty smoothly here by the time anybody remembers that our check didn't clear."

"I'm going to need some time out of the office today. He wants me to run some errands for him," stated Al.

"Oh damn! I had a list already started that I needed you to do. I need you to take the car down and get it washed and filled up with gas, and while you are down that way you could pick up some lunch at the Applebee's curbside service. But, I guess it can wait."

Ava couldn't see the murderous look on Alfred face as he turned to leave the office. "I'll be back as soon as I finish," he said, then under his breath he said, "Never, is too soon for me to be back to help *you.*"

*

"Are you still monkeying around with that crazy computer?" asked Pete.

"Yep. Isn't Dora amazing," Patrick smiled as he patted the top of the computer. "By the way, I haven't had an opportunity to tell you about Dr. Ciccone's visit."

"Dr. Coconut was here?"

"Yep. And he came in with some pretty hot information."

"Really? What was it?"

"He gave me a name. He told me that "name" had bought sodium pentobarbital from the street—no prescription."

"Who?"

"Big Al. Also known as Alfred Benedetti.

"And just where did our Dr. Coconut come up with this information?"

"He said that he'd rather not say, so we'll have to check it out."

"So what do we know about Benedetti?"

"He's working as a "bodyguard" for an Ava Grissom, who is a member at Rio Grande Country Club. I made a discreet telephone call to Paula, the cocktail waitress, who told me that Ava and Big Al were at the club the night Nicki was killed."

Pete whistled. "That's pretty interesting. You think that McGuire might be telling the truth about not killing Nicki?"

"It's worth looking into, don't you think?"

"Yep. It's worth looking into. Did you find out about the woman that was picked up with Judge Brookmeyer? Was she still in our lock-up?"

"Nope. She bonded out. I asked the locals to put out an APB and bring her back in, just for questioning. Haven't heard back from them yet." Patrick's fingers were flying over the computer keyboard. "Aha!" he said triumphantly. "Here's something else that is worth looking into."

"What?"

"Grant McGuire's folks had a pretty big farm south of town. They died thirteen years ago, but the taxes are still being paid by a family trust." His fingers again flew over the keyboard.

"I pulled up a copy of that trust, also public record, which makes Grant the sole beneficiary of the farm—but not until twenty years after the last parent passed away. The older brother inherited some property the family owned in Colorado."

"You have the address of that farm? Maybe we need to go take a look?"

"The address is in Township and Range numbers. However, there's a little grocery store in Belen. The owner has been there for fifty years and he knows where to find anything."

"What are we waiting for?" asked Pete.

"You have a court date on that gang case, remember. You are due up there in Judge Morris' courtroom in about fifteen minutes. Not only that, you have a dinner date with Carmen tonight. You are picking her up at six o'clock."

"Oh, damn! I can't break that date with Carmen, and I sure can't stand up old Judge Morris."

"Maybe I can stall for a little while."

"Stalling isn't going to buy me any time with Judge Morris," moaned Pete.

"That's true. He is quite the stickler for being on time, as well."

"And I have been working up the courage for this date with Carmen all week, ever since you suggested I give her a phone call."

"I think that she was sort of looking forward to it as well. Just to see if you had made any changes in your life style."

"Oh good grief! How do I get myself into these messes?"

"I need to call Jon Howell and let him know what information Dora had to offer. He will probably want to go with us."

"Are you thinking about going right away?"

"Wouldn't you, if you were in their shoes?"

"Oh hell. I'll never get Carmen to go out with me again if I can't even make a simple dinner date."

"I suggest you get on up to the court, and maybe it will get postponed or something. I will call Carmen and tell her that your reservations have been changed to seven-fifteen, so you'll pick her up at seven instead of six."

"But what about the Rancher's Club? I made reservations for six-fifteen."

"I doubt that will make any difference. I'll call and change your reservations and that way you'll be off the hook. Then I'll call that grocer in Belen."

"Pat, old buddy, you are a God-send," Pete almost hugged Patrick with relief.

Patrick arranged for Tom Howell and his son, Jon, to meet them at the parking lot of the super market that was right around the corner from where Carmen lived. That way, when the group got back to town, Pete would have the best chance to pick her up on time.

*

Ginger woke with a start. Her stomach had started growling again. She climbed out of the tub and slowly drank another glass of water. Now that she had a plan, she was ready to tackle the hinge bolts again. She rubbed her cold, stiff hands until they had some feeling in them, picked up the thin, metal rod and her shoe and attacked the hinge bolt with a vengeance. Thirty or forty whacks later, the first bolt was free from the middle hinge on the door.

Encouraged, she decided the bottom one would be next. She didn't have as much room to maneuver the metal rod and the shoe, so it was going to be trickier. She laid the rug on the floor by the door so that she would have something to kneel on as she tackled the job at hand.

The knuckle that had been split started bleeding again, and there was a dull ache between her shoulder blades, but she was determined to continue the attack. In the back of her mind she was worried about being able to reach the bolt in the top hinge well enough to get it out. She knew that her arms would tire quickly when they were up above her head, so she needed to conserve her energy as much as possible.

Doggedly, she hit the metal rod with the heel of her shoe. *Thank goodness I wasn't wearing high heels!*

***

In Total Darkness

Chapter Thirty-Two

Bud and Claire Simpson landed back in Albuquerque just when the Indian summer came to a screeching halt. The wind was out of the north, right off the snow that had fallen in Colorado the night before and the sun had decided it would be a good day to stay out of sight. It was completely overcast with dark clouds beginning to gather at the top of Sandia Crest.

"Let's turn around and go back to the Caribbean, Bud," whined Claire. "I don't like cold weather."

Bud shivered against the cold wind and said, "I wish we could, Honey-bun, but I've got to be in Santa Fe when the legislature opens its session, and Christmas is only a few weeks away. You want to be away from the kids during Christmas?"

Claire pulled her sweater tighter around her and resigned herself to the change of climate. "Of course not," she responded, "But let's get out of this airport and go home."

As soon as the suitcases were unloaded and carried into the house Claire got busy sorting through the mail and Bud went quickly into his office and closed the door. Pulling out his cell phone, he quickly dialed and waited for an answer.

"Welcome home," said the voice on the other end of the line.

"Is everything taken care of that you were working on when I left," Bud asked.

There was a pause on the other end of the line. "Not exactly," was the reply.

Bud didn't wait for an explanation, but simply snapped his flip-phone shut and grimaced. *You just can't get good help these days!*

*

Thankfully, the arresting officer was not able to make the court appearance so Judge Morris decided to continue the case before him until the next morning. Pete breathed a sigh of relief and raced to the elevator as soon as the judge's gavel hit the wood block.

His office was just a couple of buildings down the street from the courthouse, and Pete didn't bother with a vehicle. He ran.

When he reached Patrick's office he was wheezing pretty badly and had a "stitch" in his side. He leaned over with his hands on his knees, trying to catch his breath.

"A little bit out of shape, are we?" asked Patrick mildly.

"Stuff it, Mahoney," Pete gasped.

"You are just in time. I'm picking up the Howells in ten minutes—that's a quarter of four. The grocer in Belen gave me great directions, so we should be able to find the house with no problem. It's still going to push us to be back by seven. Are you ready?"

Breathing a little easier now, Pete replied, "Let's roll. How long do you think it will take us to get to the farm?"

"Well, the farm is actually just this side of Belen, which is thirty miles from the edge of town. Traffic shouldn't be a problem this time of day, so I'd say roughly forty-five minutes to an hour."

The two detectives picked up Tom and Jon Howell at the designated super market parking lot. There wasn't a lot of conversation on the ride, as Tom was feeling lousy, Patrick was concentrating on his driving, Pete was thinking about what he would say to Carmen, and Jon respectfully kept his silence.

*

CLINK! The last hinge bolt popped out and hit the bathroom floor. Ginger's arms were aching from having to work above her head, and her last gasp of energy was just about gone. She felt her way back over to the closed commode and sat down to catch her breath. She would have to conserve her energy for pulling the old wooden door off the hinges. *I really need something I can pry with.*

She knelt down and felt around under the pedestal of the lavatory. *There! There's a flat metal bar that attaches to the drain stopper. If I can just figure out how to get it loose!*

She sat down on the rug that she had pulled over to the pedestal, and carefully felt of all the connections. Working slowly and deliberately, she finally managed to free the flat bar from the rest of the drain.

She stuck the bar in the crack between the door and the jam, right where the hinges were attached. There was a slight movement! Gradually she worked the hinges apart, so that she now had something to hang onto while she pulled on the door. Summoning the last of her strength she jerked the door off its hinges just enough so she could crawl through the opening.

"If I could just see where I'm going, I'd be out of this dungeon." she said weakly—stumbling a bit as she felt her way along the bedroom wall.

Patrick's vehicle pulled up in front of the old farm house just about the same time that Ginger crawled through the door of the bathroom.

Pete knocked on the old front door, knowing there would not be a reply. He then used a credit card to unlock the front door and the four men entered the house.

"Why don't we spread out and see what might turn up," said Patrick.

"Good idea," said Tom.

"Look! There are fresh footprints in the dust on the floor. Someone has been here recently," cried Jon.

The four men scattered in all directions to look through the old farmhouse, checking each room carefully.

Meanwhile, Ginger felt her way through the room she had entered, discovered the door and crept along the hallway into the main room of the basement.

Am I hearing things? I thought I heard footsteps up over my head! It may be the kidnapper! I'd better be really quiet or he might put me back in that bathroom.

There seemed to be just a crack of light coming from up above. She took baby steps, with her hands stretched out in front of her as she carefully headed toward the tiny line of light. Her toes hit the bottom of a staircase, and she fell forward, bumping her elbow. She stifled a reaction by putting her hand over her mouth, and rubbed the elbow to relieve the tingling sensation.

Ginger slowly climbed up the stairs toward the thin line of light that was filtering through the bottom of the kitchen door.

Just as she got to the top step, Tom reached the door to the basement stairs, and as he pulled it open Ginger stumbled into his arms, still holding onto the knob.

"Wha…!" cried Tom. He was shocked by the apparition he was holding in his arms. Ginger's hair was dirty and hung in strings around her face. All signs of her make-up had been washed off days ago, and were replaced by smudges of dirt. There were rivulets of clear lines where her tears had left streaks, and smears of dried blood from the skinned knuckle that she had wiped across her face. Her clothes were covered in the dust that had been her constant companion for all these days. The room had bright sunlight streaming through the dusty windows, and Ginger was blinded by the sudden presence of light.

"Ginger? Is that you, sweetheart? Oh, Gin! What has he done to you?" Tom took the wraith of a woman into his arms and tenderly cradled her there.

"Tommm..." was barely audible as she spoke his name. The light blinded her and tears ran from her squinted eyes. Her head fell against his chest. She was unconscious.

"Jon! Pete! I have her! Ginger is here!" he called to the other men.

"Holy sh..." started Pete as he walked into the room and caught a glance of Ginger. "Let's get her to a hospital. Now!"

Patrick was already calling for an investigation team with directions to the old farmhouse.

"Mom! Is she all right?" Jon hurried over to his parents.

"I don't know yet, son, but she is still alive." Tom picked her up and carried her out the door. Patrick ran to open the car door for Tom, then rushed to get behind the wheel. Pete and Jon hurried into the vehicle and Patrick tore off toward I-25, full speed.

"Why don't you call for an ambulance to meet us, Pete? I'll put on the lights and siren so they can identify us."

Tom's relief at finding his wife alive was tempered by the concern he had for her condition. "We'll get you some help, Gin, just hold on a little while longer," he spoke lovingly into her ear.

***

In Total Darkness

Chapter Thirty-Three

Pete screeched to a halt in front of Carmen's front door at six fifty-nine. He raced to the door and rang the bell. Seven o'clock. On the nose!

"Hello, Carmie," he said with a swagger in his voice. "Are you ready? I have a great dinner planned—just for you and me."

Carmen looked at her watch, raised one eyebrow, and said, "Not bad, Pete. You are making progress."

"I'm sorry about making the change, but I wasn't able to get the reservation for the six-fifteen time that I had first mentioned to you." It was just a tiny little fib. "By the way, you look absolutely marvelous. Have you changed your hair style or something?"

"Thanks. Just a new haircut. And by the way, you look pretty good yourself except for a little dust on your pants leg."

Pete hastily brushed off the dust. "Well, you might be interested in knowing how I got dusty. I don't think you will be bored with our dinner conversation. You have read in the newspaper about the Howell kidnapping...." He took her elbow and ushered her to his car.

*

Meanwhile, at the hospital, Ginger had been hooked up with intravenous fluids to fight the malnutrition. She had not been able to see anything when she woke. Any light blinded her, and caused her eyes to fill with tears, so they kept the overhead lights off in her room.

They had bathed her, shampooed her hair, smoothed lotion over her chafed skin, and had attended to the cuts on her knuckles. The nurse brought heated blankets and laid them over the top of the sheets covering her.

"Oh, that's heaven," moaned Ginger. "I have been freezing to death for days."

Totally exhausted, Tom sat down in the visitor's chair by Ginger's bed, had promptly fallen asleep and began snoring loudly.

Ginger glanced over at her husband, then turned to her nurse and said, "That's the sweetest sound I've ever heard."

"Better get some sleep, yourself, Mrs. Howell. You've been through quite an ordeal," prompted the smiling nurse.

*

Struggling, Alfred Benedetti tried to think of some sort of excuse that his boss would accept. With the stakes as high as they were, it wasn't likely that *any* excuse was going to make a difference.

It was almost midnight when he pulled into the bosque and turned off his car lights. He knew he would have to be ready— for anything. He didn't have long to wait.

Bud Simpson pulled his luxury SUV up beside Al and turned off his lights. The two men got out of their cars and approached each other at the front of the vehicles.

"Al? What do you have to say for yourself?" asked Bud.

"Boss, I took care of that red-head just like you asked. Then I eliminated that woman who was arrested with the Judge, right after she bonded out of jail. She won't be a problem, and they may never find her. But—that old woman and the little kid just disappeared. I checked all of the airports, bus lines, and even the trains. They haven't left town unless someone took them as the old lady doesn't drive according to the neighbor. But no one has seen them," he was begging. He hated the way he sounded when he begged.

"The Senator was not very happy, Al," Bud's voice sounded menacing.

"Just give me a little more time! They've got to show up somewhere."

Bud's hand had moved inconspicuously toward his back. He pulled a .357 Magnum out of his waistband, aimed and fired in one swift motion. The bullet hit Al right between the eyes, just as Bud said, "Time's up!"

Bud left the body right where it dropped, blew on his gun and replaced it in his waistband. He then promptly got into his vehicle and left the bosque.

*

Early the next morning, Bud placed a call to Ava Grissom. "Looks like you are going to have to break in a new bodyguard, Ava," he said.

There was silence on Ava's end of the line, but only for a moment, as she responded, "Do you know of someone you might recommend?"

Bud ignored the question. "Why don't you let me pick you up for breakfast? I know the perfect place. They serve a breakfast meal called "Killer Huevos Rancheros". It's to *die* for."

"Sounds.... marvelous," said Ava hesitantly.

Bud made sure no one saw Ava get into his vehicle when he picked her up at the office building. Ava was still fascinated by her hands. She waved her fingers with the long, fake nails around in front of her face as she chattered.

"How was your trip? Did you and Claire enjoy the beaches and the bright sun?"

Bud glanced over at her without replying.

"It really must be beautiful this time of year, and it's so nice to get out of the cold weather."

Although it was bright daylight, there was no traffic on the road as Bud turned toward the bosque.

"I wasn't aware there were any restaurants down in this part of town," said Ava, suddenly noticing they had pulled off onto a dirt road. "Oh, look. There's Al's car! I wonder what he's doing down..." Ava stopped in mid-sentence, suddenly realizing what Bud had in mind. He stopped just short of Al's cold, stiff, body.

"Out of the car, Ava." Bud's voice was no longer friendly. It was deadly.

"Oh, please, Bud! You don't want to do this. Please!" she begged.

"OUT OF THE CAR!" he yelled.

Terrified now, Ava started begging and tears poured down her cheeks. "Bud, please. Don't do this! I've done everything that you told me to do. Everything is just getting started. We'll have a great operation and a perfect "laundry" for your money within a week or so. Please, Bud!"

"GET OUT OF THE CAR!"

"Please, please, please! You don't want to do this. I'll do anything you ask!"

Bud raised his hand with the gun in it and started to strike her in the face.

Realizing that he was not going to listen to reason and that she couldn't do anything about it, Ava opened the door, then started running toward the trees, as fast as she could go, in the ridiculous high-heeled shoes she wore.

"Bad move, bitch!" cried Bud, taking careful aim with his Magnum. The bullet tore into the back of Ava's head, dropping her in her tracks. "I told you it was *to die for!*" sneered Bud. He quickly got back into his car and drove away. As soon as he was back on the Interstate, he flipped open his cell phone and punched in a number from the stored memory.

When the telephone was answered, Bud said, "Is he there?"

"May I ask who is calling?"

"No. He will want to talk to me."

"One moment, please." The receptionist put the phone on hold. It was only a few seconds until there was an answer.

"Yeah?"

"It's all done. There won't be any problem with the two people we discussed," said Bud. "No more loose ends."

"What about the old lady?"

"She hasn't showed up. He couldn't locate her. That loose end is still out there."

"Don't leave it hanging…or it could end up hanging us."

"Don't worry, Senator. Now that I'm back in town, it will be my first priority."

***

Chapter Thirty-Four

Pete had a spring in his step as he whistled his way into his office the next morning. His dinner date with Carmen had been a big success. She had even invited him in for a nightcap when he took her home. That was as far as it went, but it was progress!

"Top o' th' mornin' to ye, lad!" Pete said to Patrick as he stuck his head in the office door.

Patrick raised both eyebrows. "That good, huh?" He rose from his desk. "She going to see you again?"

"I was afraid to push my luck. I'll try to give her a call in a day or so, and plan on another dinner date."

"I'm happy for you, and I hate to burst the bubble, but we've got problems."

Pete's smile disappeared, and he sat down with a thump. "Okay, burst my bubble. What's up?"

"Patrolman called in this morning with two bodies, down in the bosque."

Pete looked up quickly. "Not beheaded"

"No. Not beheaded. Shot. With a big gun."

"Any identification on them?"

"On one of them. Unfortunately. One of them was Alfred Benedetti."

"Big Al? The lead we had from Dr. Coco....Ciccone on the sodium pentobarbital?"

"That's the one. The other was a middle-aged woman. She didn't have any ID on her body, and no purse was found."

"So there goes our next best lead on the du Pree murder."

"Maybe. Maybe not. We have his address. We need to go check out his place. No telling what we might find there."

"Are the bodies still on the scene?"

"Yes. They were waiting to pick them up until Homicide had a chance to check it out. You ready?"

"Oh, yeah. Always ready to go look at another dead person," said Pete sarcastically. "After we look at the scene, we can check out his place."

*

The Unit for Forensic Investigation had been called and was photographing the crime scene.

"Doesn't look like there's going to be any mystery about cause of death—on either one of these bodies," remarked Pete.

Patrick leaned over Benedetti's body and quickly checked the pockets of his clothing. "This cell phone could be a valuable source of information, Pete. I'll have the UFI guys bag it up, and we'll take it with us."

"From the looks of the footprints, the lady was running from the shooter, trying to get away. Benedetti caught it smack between the eyes. That had to be a surprise," said Pete. "Am I imagining things, or is there a difference in the looks of those two bodies? Al is stiff as a board, but it doesn't appear that this lady has been dead that long."

"UFI will be able to tell us about that," said Patrick.

They obtained an address from Benedetti's wallet and drove there immediately. It was a surprisingly upscale apartment complex in the Northeast Heights.

"You got the paper work going for us to search his place?"

"With a dead body, I don't think anyone is going to complain," replied Patrick.

Mahoney and Lucero arrived at Al's apartment complex about five minutes before Bud Simpson got there. When Bud started up the steps to the apartment, he saw that the door was open and heard Lucero and Mahoney talking inside. He certainly didn't want the Homicide Detectives to find him at this location, so he quickly went back down the stairs and into his vehicle. He cursed as he drove away.

"Damn. I thought I'd have time to check out his place before they found him." He drove on past the building and back toward home. *Claire and I might need to think about getting out of town—permanently.*

"Well, what do we have here?" said Pete, pulling a plastic bag out of a dresser drawer. The bag contained a small vial marked "sodium pentobarbital", and a needle for injecting it. "We may have just found Nicki's murder weapon."

"There is also a residue of white powder in this bottom drawer. Could be cocaine. We'll have the UFI boys get a sample of this and run it.

"Wow, take a look at this Patrick, my boy. All of this paraphernalia is for weighing drugs and there is a stack of small plastic bags."

"Benedetti may be the drug dealer that Nicki overheard talking to the politician—as well as her killer."

"Was Benedetti a member of Rio Grande Country Club?"

"I don't think so, but his boss-lady was. And, according to Dr. Ciccone, that gave him access to all of the privileges of the club, as long as he was with her."

"You think that other body is his boss-lady?"

"Could be. Wonder why anyone would want them both dead?" asked Patrick.

"I don't know—maybe to tie up loose ends. But I have an idea we're going to learn something from that cell phone—unless Benedetti is more of a techno-geek than he appeared."

Patrick walked into the kitchen of the apartment and whistled. "Speaking of techno-geek, I wonder what we'll find in here." On the table there was a state of the art laptop computer.

When Lucero and Mahoney got back to the office, Patrick immediately began to inspect the cell phone that Big Al had been carrying.

"It might take a few minutes, but I'll call and get a print-out of the phone record of the calls Al made and received. In the meantime, there's a menu here that allows me to see what recent calls he has made."

Pete took a few minutes and was writing up the report about the old farmhouse, and the discovery of where Ginger Howell had been held.

Patrick made a list of three numbers from the cell phone, picked up the phone sitting on his desk and called the first number.

"You have reached the voice mail of Senator Manuel Maria Apodaca-Ramos. The Senator is unavailable at the moment, but your call is important to him. Please leave a message at the sound of the tone." He hung up without leaving a message, his eyebrows flew up, and he glanced at Pete.

"Let's try the next one," said Patrick, dialing quickly. It rang four times, and then Bud Simpson answered the phone.

"Bud Simpson here."

"Hello, Mr. Simpson, this is Patrick Mahoney. I was wondering if you could come down to the police station and identify some items for us."

"What kind of items?" asked Bud. "Claire and I just flew in from the Bahamas and we're pretty tired. Is it important?"

"Lucero seems to think so."

"Let me give you a call in the morning. How does that sound?"

Pete took the phone from Patrick. "Mr. Simpson, this is Pete Lucero. We'd really like to talk to you right away. Would you like me to send a patrolman to bring you down to the station?"

"Naw. That's all right. Just give me a few minutes. I'll grab another cup of coffee and head down that way. Must be all-fired important, if it can't wait a few hours," he complained, and then hung up.

"This gets more and more interesting. What is the other number you've got?" asked Pete.

Patrick dialed it, and got an answering machine. "The Saudi Arabian Bank of Belgium is currently closed. If you would like to leave a message for Ava Grissom, please do so after the tone."

"Looks like we have definite leads to the politician and another connection to our little Texas guy," smiled Pete.

"Yes, it is going to be interesting to hear what they have to say about being connected to a murder victim," replied Patrick.

*

Bud Simpson had driven directly home after finding the Homicide Detectives at Benedetti's apartment. He got the call from Patrick just after he had pulled into his driveway and run into the house. Now he was really in a hurry.

"Hey Claire! Where are you?"

"In here, honey. What are you doing home so early? I thought that you had business in town."

"Well, I've decided that the Bahamas might be the best place for us right now. Neither one of us likes the cold. We'll just take another extended vacation."

"Oooohhh! I love it!" replied Claire. "When do you want to go?"

"Right now. You go pack, and I'll get what I need out of the office."

"Right now, as in *this minute?*" she asked. "I'll need to cancel my hair appointment, and make sure the housekeeper knows we're going, and..." began Claire.

"We can call them from the airport, Honey. I'll go make our plane reservations right now."

Claire pulled out the suitcase from bottom of the closet. She hadn't even unpacked it from the previous trip.

"Claire, I can't seem to find my laptop. Do you know where I put it?" Bud called up the stairs.

Claire stopped dead still. "Now, don't be mad at me, Sweetie. You know that computer class I was taking? I thought I might be able to use your laptop, so I took it with me to the class so the instructor could show me how to use it."

"But we just got home. When did you take it down there?"

"The class met at eight o'clock this morning—it only lasts for forty-five minutes, and I've missed it for three weeks. I was getting so far behind! You went out for breakfast, so I went to the class."

"You stup..." he stopped, not wanting to upset Claire. "That's okay; just tell me where you put it when you got home." Bud hurriedly went up the stairs to the bedroom where Claire was packing.

"I didn't bring it home with me." Tears began to well up in Claire's eyes.

"What!" Bud's voice was rising and he was beginning to panic. "What did you do with the damned computer?"

"I left it with the instructor! Oh, please, Bud, don't be angry with me. When I was in the class this morning, I guess I pushed some wrong buttons on the keyboard, and I got it locked up. The instructor had another class, but he said he would be able to fix it. I thought that I'd have time to go back down there and get it before you even missed it. Don't be angry, please!"

Bud looked at his watch. "Okay, we may still have enough time. You come with me right now. We're going back to that class and get my computer from that instructor. Let's go!" Bud picked up the suitcase in one hand and grabbed Claire's wrist in the other.

"I don't think that he will be there by now," whined Claire. "His other class met right after mine did, and he was going to take the computer with him down to the University of New Mexico, check it out, and call me where to meet him. If we leave now, we'll miss his call."

Bud started pacing back and forth. The information in that computer could send him to prison for the rest of his life. He had been so careful to keep it out of Claire's reach, but with the problem of Big Al and Ava on his neck, he must have forgotten to put it back up on the top shelf of the closet. Bad mistake! Really bad!

"Okay. Here's what we will do. We'll go ahead and put the suitcases in the car and head toward UNM. We'll put the phone on call forwarding to my cell phone, so that when the instructor calls, you can tell him that we're already on the way."

"Okay, Baby, I'm sorry. I just wanted you to be proud of me."

*

The computer instructor was Native American, very good at his job, and extremely intelligent. He was also very patriotic, having been raised by his father, a Navajo Code Talker in WWII. He had been to many ceremonies where the Code Talkers had been honored, and he took pride in his father's accomplishments.

When he got back to his office after the second computer class, the first thing he did was to take a look at the laptop computer Mrs. Simpson had managed to lock down.

It didn't take but a couple of minutes for him to get the laptop up and running again. He opened each program, just to make sure they were all operating properly, when something caught his eye.

There was a folder titled "Tribes". Curious, he clicked on the folder to see what files it contained. It was a listing of Native American tribes. Intrigued, he opened one of the files, and was startled to see a dollar amount listed beside each tribal name. The dollar amount was PAC money, given by the tribe and entrusted to Bud Simpson, as a registered lobbyist. But there were two listings. One list showed the money donated to the Political Action Committee for each candidate, and the second list showed the actual disbursement of those funds. There were discrepancies of hundreds of thousands of dollars between the two lists.

Not believing what he was seeing, the instructor opened several other files. Another list was an accounting of grams of cocaine and other drugs, the amount of money paid for them, and the amount of money received for them, along with the names of the sellers and the buyers. The instructor's hands started sweating.

What the hell should I do with this information! When Mr. Simpson finds out his computer is missing, he'll come after me. I've got to get out of here. Right now!

He closed the laptop, shoved it into the carrying case, grabbed his coat, locked the door to his office, and ran to his car. He called 911 on his cell phone and asked for the FBI. The operator connected him immediately. He quickly explained the situation to the agent, and was given directions to the nearest field office. He was more than happy to toss this hot potato.

*

Bud Simpson and his wife were almost to the University of New Mexico campus, and there had been no telephone call from the instructor. Bud rolled down the window of the car and stopped a student walking by to ask for directions to the computer instructor's office.

"There are never any parking spaces on campus, Bud, and you have to have a sticker just to stop at one of these lots. The Campus Police patrol these areas like crazy," said Claire.

"This won't take but a minute," he replied. "You can stay in the car and handle anyone that gives you a problem about the double parking."

"He should have called by now," whined Claire, wringing her hands.

Bud's eyes were steely cold, and his teeth were clenched as he looked for the building. "You have no idea what you have done, you idiot! If I don't get that laptop back in my possession before that instructor starts poking around in it, I could go to prison for the rest of my life. We were leaving the country, but now it may be for good."

Claire's mouth dropped open; she looked at Bud, then just closed her mouth and didn't say anything for a moment. Tears welled up in her eyes and finally she asked, "What on earth have you been up to, Bud Simpson? I thought that you might have a list of your girlfriend's telephone numbers in it! Like a little black book! I thought that was why you tried to hide it from me all the time."

"Tried to hide it from you? What do you mean?"

"Oh, just the way you would stick it up high on the shelves and leave it locked up in a cabinet out in the motor home. What would be a better place to keep your girlfriends telephone numbers?"

"What makes you think there were "girl friends"?

"Don't be silly, Bud! Wives just know these things. I can hardly blame you, looking at that drop-dead gorgeous cocktail waitress. I only have to look in the mirror to see why you'd want to fool around with her." Tears were rolling down Claire's cheeks.

Bud turned to his wife and realized that she was a lot smarter than he gave her credit. "Honey, I love you more than life itself, and none of those little flings amounted to anything. But right now, this is serious business. We've got to get that computer back, right now, and we've got to be on the next flight back to the Bahamas. Not only that, those two snooping Homicide Detectives called and I'm supposed to be heading down to their office to identify something or other.

When they found the computer instructor's office building, Bud ran up to the door, and found it locked. When he knocked and got no response, he kicked the door, swore, and ran back to the car. They immediately left for the Albuquerque International Airport.

***

Chapter Thirty-Five

Federal agents from the Drug Enforcement Agency were waiting at the airport when Bud and Claire Simpson walked up to the ticket counter. They had been contacted after the laptop computer had been delivered to the FBI.

"Bud Simpson?" asked a DEA agent as Bud pulled out his Visa card.

Surprised, Bud turned quickly, thought about running, but changed his mind. "Yes, I'm Simpson."

"I'm with the DEA. You are under arrest for drug trafficking. Both of you will have to come with us."

After Bud and Claire were questioned, Claire was released from custody and not charged. Bud was booked into detention without bail. After a compete inspection of his laptop computer, Bud was not only charged with the drug violations, but several crimes relating to the misuse of the PAC money donated by the various Tribes.

The lobbying scandal made national headlines when it was discovered that Bud had been skimming from the tribal contributions, and the amount was in the hundreds of thousands of dollars.

When the DEA finished their investigation, the Homicide Division of the Albuquerque Police Department requested that Simpson also be held pending charges from them.

Eventually, the cyber and forensic evidence tied Bud Simpson to the killing of Alfred Benedetti and Ava Grissom. The bullets that killed them were matched to his .357 Magnum which had only his fingerprints on it, and when he was arrested, gunpowder residue was found on his hand. Bud was indicted on drug charges in addition to the first degree murders of Al Benedetti and Ava Grissom. After all of these charges, Bud confessed that he had ordered Alfred Benedetti to murder Nicolette DuPree.

Pete Lucero and Patrick Mahoney made an unannounced visit to the office of New Mexico State Senator Manuel Maria Apodaca-Ramos. When he was confronted with the information that tied him to the drug-dealing Alfred Benedetti, he was only too willing to tell all he knew—if they would cut him a deal. He denied having anything at all to do with Big Al's death or that of Ava Grissom.

*

Tom Howell walked into Ginger's office with a handful of papers. They had both recovered tremendously since the rescue.

"Whatcha got there, Babe," she asked.

"Well, you know how our daughter, Leslie, and her husband have been trying to have a baby, but have had no luck? These papers will enable them to be considered as adoptive parents for Trey du Pree."

"Oh, Tom! That's wonderful! I've always wanted a little redheaded grandbaby. You know that my redheaded mother would have been very pleased as well—not that she wouldn't have been pleased with the three wonderful grandkids that are already in the family."

Tom laughed. "I think I know what you are talking about, even if you are stepping all over your tongue."

"What about Bertha?"

"Don't you think that Leslie would like to have a nanny for her little boy?"

"That's perfect! When will we know for sure?"

"The court is pretty strict about adoptive parents. They will have to fill out all the papers, have a few personal interviews, and meet all the other criteria, but maybe I can pull some strings and help it along a bit."

"Speaking of babies, did Patrick tell you that his wife is expecting their first one?"

"No kidding! That's great. We'll have another little Irish bairn running around here before long. Is Pete going to be the godfather?"

Ginger giggled. "I have no idea, but if Carmen considers moving back home and bringing the kids, he might be a good candidate."

"It's a rough profession. The kind of stress that we had, they live with twenty-four hours a day. It's pretty rough on family life."

Tom looked closely at his wife's face. "Are you sure you are feeling well enough to be at work? That was quite an ordeal you went through, and I don't think you should push it."

"Oh, I'm fine. That seven pounds I lost was only temporary. I've already gained two of them back."

"Well, what do you say about cutting out of here and helping you gain another pound or two?"

"What do you have in mind?"

"Maybe the Rancher's Club?"

Tom and Ginger stopped for a moment to enjoy a spectacular December sunset as they left the building. Low clouds were deep burgundy, giving way to dark orange and pink, with the lower part of the clouds streaked with gold.

"Makes you wonder if Grant will ever be able to enjoy a sight like this again, doesn't it?" asked Ginger.

"He turned out to be a first-class creep," replied Tom. "I'm not at all sorry about him spending the next thirty years behind bars. Even with good behavior he's still going to do a long stretch of time."

"At least he should be able to kick the alcohol and drug habits while he's behind bars. Were you surprised that he wasn't the one that killed Nicki?"

"No. Not really. I was shocked he had guts enough to try kidnapping. I don't really think he intended to hurt me, and certainly not Sydney, when he cut the brake line. The law calls it attempted murder. The arson was really a dirty move on his part. Every time I smell that acrid smoky stink I'm going to wish I'd hit him more than once. And, I'll never forgive him for what he put you through."

"I think he was really in love with Nicki, just like Mike Stevens and Dr. Ciccone were, don't you?"

"Love? I'm not sure that Grant is capable of it."

Driving over to the restaurant, the conversation continued.

"By the way, Sweetheart, what ever happened to all of the furnishings in Ava's office?" asked Tom.

"That was no problem at all. She hadn't paid for a single item in that entire office. After she was killed I notified the people that had been sending second and third notices, and they all came and "repossessed" what was theirs. And by the way, we have a new tenant in that space now—a nice little gray-haired real estate salesman."

"Did you check his references?"

"You darn tootin' I did!"

"Well, I have some good news for you. I'm selling the office building. An offer came in on it this morning that looks pretty good."

"That really *is* good news!"

During dinner the talk turned to the upcoming Christmas holiday.

"Only a few more days until Christmas. Where has the time flown? I can't believe that we missed Brandon's football banquet. And did you hear that Sydney's cast is supposed to come off this week? Not only that, but "J' is already working out with the wrestling team. That season will start in January."

"Speaking of Christmas, are you interested in going to the Snow White Ball at Rio Grande Country Club? Maybe we can get back into a normal routine again."

"Normal sounds pretty good, doesn't it." Ginger leaned over and kissed her husband on the cheek. "How about we go home and have a "normal" evening?"

After they got into bed, Tom switched off the lamp on the nightstand and pulled Ginger over into the "spoon" of his embrace. It was very quiet for a minute, and then in a still, small, voice, Ginger said, "Tom".

"Uh huh?"

"Do you think we could keep the light on?"

The End

ABOUT THE AUTHOR

Gloria Dial Hightower was born in a very small town in West Texas. She attended school in Farwell, Texas where she graduated as Valedictorian. She met her husband, Tommy Hightower during her first semester of college at Eastern New Mexico University in Portales, New Mexico. She finished her education at Western New Mexico University in Silver City, New Mexico where she graduated with honors, receiving the Cardinal Key Award.

During her varied career she worked for a short time at a newspaper and a radio station; taught school; worked in marketing; ran her own interior decoration business; was a full-charge bookkeeper; and corporate Secretary-Treasurer.

This is the second murder mystery she has written. The first one, *The Cotton Rope Strangler,* was very well received. Her interests other than writing include church, family, oil painting, writing and performing music, and gardening. She is an avid golfer.

Since this is the third edition of *In Total Darkness,* Gloria has written another murder mystery, *The Shadow Mountain Murders,* also with Tom and Ginger Howell; and a historical fiction book called *Simon of Cyrene.*

Made in the USA
Middletown, DE
25 February 2025